D0605539

Crossing Shattuck Bridge

ALSO BY ANNETTE SANFORD

Lasting Attachments (1987)

Crossing
Shattuck Bridge

Stories by
Annette Sanford

SOUTHERN METHODIST UNIVERSITY PRESS
Dallas

These stories are works of fiction. Names, characters, places, and incidents are either the product of the author's imagination or are used fictitiously.

Copyright © 1999 by Annette Sanford
First edition, 1999
All rights reserved

Requests for permission to reproduce material from this work should be sent to:
    Rights and Permissions
    Southern Methodist University Press
    PO Box 750415
    Dallas, Texas 75275-0415

Some of the stories in this collection previously appeared in the following publications: "Crossing Shattuck Bridge," as "Crossing Shattuck Bridge the Twelfth of December," in *Southwest Review* (1992); "Strangers and Pilgrims" in *Writer's Forum* (1994); "Fo Nut X" in *Story* (1991); "Helens and Roses" in *American Short Fiction* (1992) and *New Stories from the South* (1993); "Goose Girl" in *New Stories '95, New Stories from the South* (1996), and *Continental* (1997); "Bear the Dead Away" in *The Ohio Review* (1993); "Housekeeping" in *Southwest Review* (1998); "In the Little Hunky River" in *The Chattahoochee Review* (1997) and *New Stories from the South* (1998).

Jacket photograph: Sanford Bridge, Jackson County, Texas, by Richard Korczynski

Jacket design: Tom Dawson and Bill Planey
Text design: Bill Planey

LIBRARY OF CONGRESS CATALOGING-IN-PUBLICATION DATA

Sanford, Annette.
    Crossing Shattuck Bridge : stories / by Annette Sanford. — 1st ed.
        p.   cm.
    Contents: Mr. Moore's old car — Crossing Shattuck Bridge — Strangers and pilgrims — Fo nut X — Helens and roses — Goose girl — Bear the dead away — The oil of gladness — Housekeeping — In the little hunky river.
    ISBN 0-87074-442-9 (cloth)
    1. United States—Social life and customs—20th century Fiction. I. Title.
PS3569.H5792C76   1999
813'.54—dc21   99-23578

Printed in the United States of America on acid-free paper

10   9   8   7   6   5   4   3   2   1

For Louis, Anna, and Mary

Contents

Mr. Moore's Old Car

MR. MOORE lived with his mother across the alley from our house, down on the corner.

When I played in the alley he was always polite. "Molly, how are you?"

"I'm fine, Mr. Moore."

"How is your mother?"

"She's fine. How is yours?"

Old Mrs. Moore had white hair and a cane. She was sixty. Or eighty. "And how old are you?" She had hold of my arm on a bright winter day.

"Ten," I said.

"Are you married?"

"No, ma'am."

She was married, she said, once upon a time. She set her head like a bird's. "He was gassed in France."

I hurried home with that. "What did she mean?"

"She meant her son, not her husband," said Nora, my aunt, who had bobbed her hair and looked like a crane.

"He was killed in the war," Johanna, my mother, said. "Gas was the weapon."

"Was it shot from a gun?"

"In a manner of speaking." Johanna was primping. Lipstick and powder and toilet water.

"Was Mr. Moore's brother older or younger?"

"Molly," my mother said.

"Older," said Nora. I liked her hair, but her husband didn't. He told her, Don't cut it, and she went ahead anyway.

"What was his name?"

"Thurmond," Johanna said.

"Bertram," said Nora.

I lay down on the bed and looked at a painting of ducks on a pond, "Was Mr. Moore ever married?"

"I don't think he was."

"Do you think he was, Nora?"

"No, I do not." She put on her school coat. "Who would have Mr. Moore?"

"Nora!" Johanna said.

"Johanna?" said Nora. She went out the door. My mother left too. They were going to the dressmaker and then to the store.

"Can I go?" I asked

"No," said Johanna. "You can go to the picture show." She gave me a dime, and a nickel for candy.

I went out to the kitchen to talk to Berniece. Berniece, the cook and the Grand High Matron of the African Sisterhood. Berniece was tall and wore canvas shoes with the toes cut out to make room for her corns.

"Are you making a cake?"

"Do it look like I am?" She made flat, heavy cakes. With lard, Nora said. With lead, said my father.

"Is the cake for supper?"

"Must be," said Berniece, "since we done had our dinner."

I sat on a stool. "Do you know about gas?"

"Gas," she said. "I reckon I do."

"They used gas in the war and blew up soldiers."

"I never heard that."

"My mother told me."

"Stop bumping your feets on my cabinet doors."

"I wasn't," I said, and stopped at once. "Can I taste that, Berniece?"

"If you want to get worms."

"Worms!" I said.

"That's why we got stoves." She stood back from the bowl. "Come here and stir. And don't knock nothin over." She went out to the pantry for a dip of snuff. Wet, brown stuff she kept tucked in her lip.

"Berniece," I called. "Were you ever married?"

"You stir that cake."

"Were you, Berniece?"

"How could I be? I got too much sense to tie down to that." She came back to the kitchen. "Give me that spoon and move over yonder."

"Nora's got sense—enough to teach algebra—and she got married." To Howard the Science Teacher, but they had no baby. They might never have a baby, Johanna said. She said not to mention it or Nora would cry.

"What's wrong with getting married?" I asked Berniece.

"Nothin if you wants to. Everthing if you don't."

"I think I'd like to."

"Hop to it then."

"I'm not old enough yet."

"You fourteen, aren't you?"

"Berniece! I'm ten."

"You still only ten?" She poured yellow batter into a pan. "Reach me that towel. You got everthing sticky."

"Mr. Moore could have married, but he never did. Do you know Mr. Moore?"

"Hershey Kiss Moore? Or Mr. T-Bone Moore?"

"Mr. Moore on the corner."

"Oh, that one," she said. "Got that rusting-down car." His car in the alley that we saw every day when we sat at our table. No tires, no roof, no running board either.

I said to Berniece, "I found a chicken egg in it."

"Could've found lots worse."

"I found it in the front where the driver sits down."

"He don't sit there no more. That car been parked there since before you were born."

"Why has it?" I asked.

"Why do the wind blow? It want to, that's why. Git outta the way." She shoved her cake in the oven.

"Mr. Moore on purpose let his car rust down?"

"Drove it up there, didn't he? And walked off and left it?"

"Did you see him, Berniece?"

"Most likely I did. Hadn't I always been standing here front of this window?"

"Did he have a garage then?"

"Had it same as now. That say something, don't it?"

I leaned on my elbow. "What does it say?"

"Say something the matter with him, let a garage stand empty and a car rot down."

"Do cars rot like bananas?"

"They rots like rust! Now go along, Molly. Go somewheres else."

I went down the alley to look at the car. It sat in weeds, its back end in a puddle. Rain fell on it. It never went anywhere.

"You pitiful car." I walked all around it. "You need a name."

I scooped up water. "I christen you Curtis." After Curtis Cooper, a boy in my grade.

I climbed up and sat down where the egg was laid.

Old Mrs. Moore came out on her porch. "Thurmond! Bertram!" She hollered again. "Where are you, boys?"

I went through the fence gap and into her yard.

She was out on the steps. Her hair was a mess, all stringing down. "Have you seen my boys?"

"No ma'am, I haven't." But I knew where one was, the one that was gassed that she thought was her husband. "Do you need anything that I can do?"

"Are you a nurse?"

"No ma'am, I'm a child, but I might could help. Or I'll run get Berniece if she hasn't gone home."

"Come in right now. Come into the house!"

Her cat's head was stuck in a salmon can.

When we opened the door it was clawing the drapes down. Around on the floor was everything it had broken.

"Catch her!" Mrs. Moore said.

"I'll see if I can."

I chased her all over, in and out of rooms I wanted to look at, but didn't have time to. There were pictures galore. I saw Nora in one.

I ran past Mrs. Moore. "Is that Nora?" I said.

"Who?" She was fanning, lying back in a chair.

"That girl in the photograph." I ran back and got it.

"See to the cat!" was all she could tell me.

Mr. Moore came in. "What's happening in here?"

I caught hold of his arm. "The cat stuck her head in a salmon can."

We both ran together. "Is that Nora?" I asked.

He grabbed up a shawl and captured the cat. "Hold onto this. I'll go get a hammer."

I couldn't hold on. The cat got loose, but he caught her again. He held the can with one hand and hammered with the other until he bent it crossways and her head popped out. She staggered around and went under the couch.

"Well, Molly," he said, "you saved the day." He was scratched and bleeding on his arms and his hands.

"Where is Bertram? Where is Thurmond?" old Mrs. Moore said.

"Which one are you?" I felt I could ask.

"I'm Henley," Mr. Moore said, and went after bandages.

"Is this Nora?" I said when he came back again.

He looked at the picture: my aunt and a man on the hood of a car. "Nora?" he said. "Why no, that's your mother."

"This girl is my mother? Who is this hugging her?"

"Oh, well," Mr. Moore said. "It seems to be me."

I came to the supper table ready to tell. I said, "Mr. Moore's cat caught her head in a salmon can."

"Not now," said Johanna. "We're having a toast." Howard and Nora. Johanna and Dad.

"Where is my toast?"

"Here, use your water."

"To Nora," my father said, raising his glass.

Nora turned pink.

"And to Howard," Johanna said.

"And the baby!" said Howard, pinker than Nora.

"What baby?" I asked.

Nora gave me a squeeze. "The one we're expecting."

What they did in town was to go to the doctor. It was coming in June, the doctor said. He said Nora was fine.

"Nora is fine!" Howard said. He waved his glass in the air and spilled wine on the table.

"And isn't she beautiful!" he said after that. Her hair, too, it seemed, since he smoothed his hand over it. And he kissed her right there, not caring who saw him.

I thought I'd be happy. We wanted a baby. But instead I was sad, sad and mad and prickling all over like the time I had hives from too many crabs.

"What will you name her?" Johanna said.

"June," I offered.

"June!" Nora laughed.

"Or Junior," I said.

"Junior is worse!"

I ran from the room, boohooing loudly.

"What's the matter with her?" I heard from the pantry where I flopped on the floor.

"Hurt feelings," said Howard.

"Jealous?" said Nora.

"Probably tired," Johanna said. "Those cowboy shows affect her that way."

"I didn't go to the show!" I yelled from my hideout.

If anyone loved me they'd know where I was: up in a tree for three or four hours, watching Mr. Moore as he came and went.

I wasn't called back when the cake was served, but I heard Nora say, "Why, it's fluffy and light!"

What was light, said my father, was Nora's head.

They left after that, Nora and Howard, to go to their house. Before Nora was married, when she lived with us, they put out the lights when they kissed on the couch.

I said to Johanna when I was going to bed, "I guess when you're married you can kiss anywhere."

"Within limits," she said and put her hand on my forehead.

"I don't have a fever. I'm out of sorts."

"We won't worry, then. You'll feel better tomorrow."

"I won't like Howard any better tomorrow."

She turned down the bed. "You've always loved Howard."

"I didn't tonight. He was silly and stupid. And Nora," I said, "was so full of that baby."

Johanna laughed. "She isn't full yet, but before long she will be."

"Did you kiss Mr. Moore?"

"What?" she said. She had her head in a drawer, hunting pajamas.

"He had his arm around you."

"Who?" She stood up.

"Mr. Henley Moore."

"Oh heavens," she said and sat down on my pillow.

"Their cat caught its head in a salmon can. I went in their house and helped get it out."

"What else?" she asked.

"It ran through the rooms and I saw all the pictures. I saw yours in a frame up on the dresser. You were all snuggled up with Mr. Moore."

She looked at the ceiling. "Oh Nora, I need you."

"Did he ask you to marry him?"

"No, he did not. Well, later on he did, in a roundabout way."

I cried again. "What about Daddy?"

"Molly." She held me. "This can all be explained."

"You were off by yourself with Mr. Moore! There were bushes behind you and part of a river."

"It was a Sunday School picnic. Mr. Moore was the teacher."

I caught a glimpse of that: Mr. Moore in a suit, reading the Bible.

"—and we weren't alone. Someone else was right there, someone taking the picture."

"Who? Was it Daddy?"

"It was Nora," she said.

"Where was Daddy?"

"Swimming, I think, with somebody else."

"A girl?"

"Yes, a girl. From out of town."

We both lay down and got under the covers.

"Are you hungry?" she said. "I fixed you a plate."

I wanted cake, but how would I swallow it? "Why was Daddy swimming with another girl?"

"Sweetheart," she said, "we weren't always married."

"Where was everyone else?"

"Eating and swinging on grapevine swings."

"Was Nora in a picture with Mr. Moore?"

"Sadly, she wasn't. She had a crush on Mr. Moore, but was too shy to show it."

"Did he care about Nora?"

"He liked her, of course, but not in that way."

The way he liked Johanna, and still did, I said. "He always asks me in the alley, How is your mother?"

"You ask about his mother. It's the polite thing to do."

My father came in. "Is this about over?"

"Not quite," said Johanna.

"It's ten o'clock, Jo."

"We'll be through in a minute."

When he went in the bathroom, I said to Johanna, "Did you hug Mr. Moore to make Daddy jealous?"

"I think I did, but I don't think I knew it."

"Poor Mr. Moore," I said. "Poor Nora, too."

"Come on," said Johanna. "Let's go in the kitchen."

She brought out my plate from the warming oven. Baked chicken and gravy. Potatoes and peas.

"Do I get any cake?"

"Maybe later."

"It's awful," I said. "Daddy and you."

"I know it seems awful, but really it isn't. It's the way things are done."

"Everyone does it?"

"In varying degrees. Let's do have cake." She got up and sliced it. "And a glass of milk too."

She sat down again. "You see, that's how it happens. It's how I found Daddy and Daddy found me."

"You weren't lost from each other."

"How we fell in love, I mean. You find out who you love by going out with people you never can love."

"I don't think I will."

"Wait till you're older."

"How old were you then?"

"Seventeen. Eighteen."

I ate my cake slowly. "If Nora's crush on Mr. Moore had turned into something, she would have married him and not married Howard."

"It couldn't turn into something," my mother said. "The man Nora needed was not Mr. Moore. It was someone like Howard."

"Did she know that then?"

"Deep down she did."

I was falling asleep.

"I'll tell you something else." She patted my cheek. "You will still be Nora's girl if she has three babies."

"How do you know?"

"She told me so. And Howard said this: he said give you a kiss."

"He kisses everybody."

"He didn't kiss me."

We went back to my room and I got into bed. "Was that Mr. Moore's old car you were hugging him on?"

"It wasn't old then." She turned out the light. "It was Mr. Moore's brother's, who was gassed in the war."

"Thurmond or Bertram?"

"Whichever one it was who wasn't his father."

When I went out to breakfast Berniece was there, wiping crumbs off the table. "Who been eating my cake in the middle of the night?"

"Me," I said. "I had to eat late because I couldn't eat early."

"What was you doing? Going around asking questions?"

"I was saving a cat."

She went out for snuff. Then I told her about it. And about Nora's baby and leaving the table.

"Sound like to me you got yourself in a snit."

"I'm all right today." I sat on the stool. "And I know a few things I didn't know yesterday."

"Hoo!" said Berniece. "This bacon I'm frying done popping all over!"

"Could I have some, please? Two slices of bacon and one slice of toast. I had a toast last night made out of water.

Berniece," I said, "do you know about love? The falling in kind?"

"What I know I ain't telling."

"Do you know about this?" I explained how it's done when you're finding out who to marry.

"Huh," said Berniece. "Mr. T-Bone Moore gonna sure be surprised."

"Mr. Henley Moore was in love with my mother."

"Say he was," said Berniece. "That rusty car man?"

"It was his cat I saved."

"Did you ask why he done it?"

"Why he let his car rot? I didn't have time. But I figured it out."

"Tell me tomorrow."

"Why not today?"

"I about had enough for this Sunday morning."

"Just one more thing."

"Well, hurry it up."

I made her sit down and brought the toast and the bacon. While we ate I talked. "Mr. Moore," I said, "left the car in the alley because it belonged to his brother and when his brother was gassed it made him feel so bad he parked it there and gave up driving forever."

Berniece poured her coffee. "This be the man hit the cat with the hammer?"

"He didn't hit the cat. He was bending the can."

"Wonder this morning do she know the difference."

"Or—" I went on.

"Or what?" said Berniece, gathering dishes. "One thing, that's all, and you already said it."

"That was only the first part. Now you have to guess what else could have happened." I followed her to the sink. "I'll give you a hint. Think about love."

"I'm thinking about a pork roast got to go in the oven."

"Mr. Moore, remember, was in love with my mother."

Berniece ran water till I couldn't stand it. "Guess, Berniece!"

"I guess it might could've been when your mama wouldn't have him he throwed the keys in the river and there it sits."

I jumped up and down. "Yes! That's it!"

"Naw, it ain't. That ain't the half of it."

"What do you mean?"

"You just scratchin the top. What about what's under?" She handed me a dish towel. "Dry these plates."

I had to dry the cups, too, before she would finish.

"Don't it seem mighty funny he stopped at keys? He could of run the whole thing down in the river."

I sat again on the stool. "But he didn't," I said.

"Didn't," said Berniece, "because he got bigger plans. He going to park that car in just the right spot so your mama have to look at it ever day of her life."

"That's awful, Berniece!"

"Sure awful for old Moore. He don't even know that by now she don't see it."

"I wish you hadn't told me."

"Then look at it this way." She turned her back on me. "He might of just wore out, driving that car. Or," she said and made a hiccuping sound, "he could of drove it up there and ran out of gas."

"Are you laughing?" I said. "Why are you laughing?"

"Got a little tickle down my throat."

"Snuff," I said.

"Might be it."

"Are you laughing at me?"

She broke out in cackles. "No, sugar lump. I'm laughing at love."

"The falling in kind?"

"That kind too."

"I don't think it's funny." I got down off the stool. "Tell my mother I've gone to Sunday school."

"I will," said Berniece, "and while you're at it, stop by those Moores' and see did that cat get up for breakfast."

Crossing Shattuck Bridge

THE DAY got really dark about one o'clock Monday. A foglike mist shut down the sky, and the only thing stirring out in the yard was a little green bird—an orange-crowned warbler—scavenging the roots of the sycamore. In heaps on the lawn lay our old white bedspreads, put out on the weekend to keep the freeze off the flowers. The flowers froze anyway—the cold was so intense—but we left the spreads there in disgust and dismay for the sun to dry. Then it never appeared.

Bob, at loose ends with a crick in his back from slipping down on the terrace, had finally settled down by the double windows to read about Jamaica, where he thinks we should go, and then the fog came in and he had to switch on the lamp.

"If it's going to rain," he said, "I wish it would do it." This was spoken in the voice that means he needs cheering up, but I didn't respond. I needed cheering myself because of one or two things I had on my mind.

A woman, for one, dying in Cottertown and I hadn't gone to the funeral.

Katie wanted me to go in spite of the cold spell. She rang up on Saturday as I was finishing my hair, trying to get it dry before the blizzard blew in and gave me pneumonia.

"You don't think you'll go? Why, Sibby," she said. Sibyl is my name, but she still calls me Sibby from our school days in Cottertown—so long ago now they seem in my mind like scenes from a play. "Marian Lewis practically raised us."

I felt ashamed of myself. That's Katie's effect on me half the time. My relationship with her is still locked into childhood. Press the childhood button and Katie is the boss. But I'm afraid of icy roads and of losing control, and I didn't yield.

"It's only forty miles," Katie insisted. "We could walk if we had to." She has inflated ideas of how fit she is because she exercises in all kinds of weather and rides a bike in her living room and heaven knows what. It's a subject I avoid if I possibly can.

"I can't go, Katie." And I hung up the phone. Bob applauded my valor, but of course she rang back, and in the end I said I'd go. I even got so far as putting on my black shoes with the death-defying heels, and a layer of sweaters under my coat, but before I got my purse out the sleet began falling the worst I'd ever seen. The worst, Bob said, that it ever had fallen. The phone went out and the lights did too, and nobody went anywhere.

The next thing was we didn't have any water. I mean it quit running. Our pipes were wrapped, but the town pump is electric.

"We should have thought of that," Bob kept saying. "I can't understand it, stuck without water." Blaming me.

Oh, he wasn't, I know, but I'm sensitive about water—about thirst in particular—and to mention it, even, seemed crass to me. We weren't really desperate. We had milk and juice, and water in a bottle I keep for the iron, though I don't know as I'd drink it. Or let him drink it either.

I didn't have to find out because we went on to sleep, after a fashion, and by noon the next day the power was on.

Katie called on Monday as soon as the thaw came. I was watching the warbler when the telephone rang.

"They haven't buried her yet."

"They haven't?" I said. Naturally they hadn't. If the weather had immobilized us forty miles away, it had immobilized Cottertown, but I hadn't thought it through while I moped around, thinking of other things. "When will the service be?"

"Four o'clock today. Shall I stop by and get you?"

Katie lives nearby. After Felix died we thought she might move away to be near her son, but she stayed where she was. Because of me, Bob says, and I expect that's true.

"Four o'clock?" I said. "I'll be ready at two."

Bob put down Jamaica when I hung up the phone. "What was that all about?"

When I told him he said, "You ought not to go. You showed better sense on Saturday."

"It was sleeting on Saturday."

"It's pea soup today. You'll be late coming back. You might have an accident."

I thought we might too, but I put on my flat shoes instead of high heels and when Katie honked I went on anyway.

Luckily for us, the fog thinned out. A spot like an oyster cracker showed where the sun was. "Look," Katie said, "it's clearing up."

She mentioned going to visit Marian the middle of last summer. Marian, the woman we were going to see buried. "She still had her Christmas tree up in the parlor. And foam rubber fruit in a bowl on the table."

"She's slipping," I said, forgetting for a minute she had slipped all the way. Afterward I kept thinking of Marian dead as we drove along.

The road to Cottertown is fairly exciting. It's paved for a stretch and then for six miles it's nothing but gravel. You go over Shattuck Bridge, which ought to be marked *One Way for Bicycles*. It's so narrow, I mean. A rusty old thing with flooring planks missing every few feet. It's due to be replaced when the county gets the money, but it hasn't happened yet, in thirty-five years.

When you get past the bridge, you see deer sometimes, and wild turkeys and armadillos. We ran over a skunk once, but not on the day we were headed for the funeral.

The woman who was dead, Marian Lewis, looked after Katie and me when we were nine years old, coming into town, going to school. We lived out on Box Road, twelve miles in the country. Our fathers were widowers. Our mothers died the same week—on the same day, in fact—from yellow jaundice. Hepatitis, it's called now. They got it from drinking well-water one day on a picnic they took us on.

They were young pretty women as I remember them, coming out of the house, laughing and talking, with the lunch in a basket. Meatloaf sandwiches and lemonade. The men, our fathers, were off cutting hay. Katie and I were making mud pies, slicing Jerusalem cherries to decorate the tops, and baking them in jar lids out in the sun.

A few snipey people got it started in town that our mothers acted foolishly because they were drunk, which wasn't the truth. They were sampling dewberry wine they had put up themselves, but as Bob points out, the alcohol content was bound to be nil. Wine made by women never gathers much strength. Never has a chance to, according to Bob. They dive right into it, right off the vine.

Well, the upshot was: the lemonade spilled.

It wasn't clear how, just the jar tipped over and emptied itself onto the quilt where we were having our lunch.

It didn't matter to me, or Katie either. We had drunk our fill while we were eating our sandwiches. But our mothers had a thirst, a clawing thirst from the wine they'd had. Walking home in the sun, they joked about camels. At a broken-down house where nobody lived they searched out a well. Within a month's time they were sick in their beds. The day they died they were yellow as mustard.

On occasions like a funeral, if you've come from a distance, you stand around talking. The first thing you know the sun has gone down—if it's shining at all, which it wasn't in Cottertown for Marian Lewis.

When we finally got going, Katie switched on the car lights and said about Marian, "She looked awfully nice."

I knew what she meant. They had held Marian over because of the weather, and as Katie said next, sometimes that works and sometimes it doesn't. We both knew of preachers who tell awful tales of preaching beside caskets of people held over.

In our mothers' case they were buried at once for fear of infection. The friend who dressed them—Marian Lewis—was told to wear gloves, and a bandana handkerchief over her nose.

In the car driving home, we talked about Marian. We lived with her for nearly two years. Three school terms and part of another. Our room in her attic looked out on the dog pound—and on down the road, on the baseball field. If we were rowdy up there she knocked on her ceiling. If we got too quiet she came up the stairs and flushed our chocolate cigarettes down the toilet. Every Tuesday night she scrambled calf brains for supper, and when she pulled on her stockings, little puffs of dust went out from the toes.

She loved pretty things. China flowers in vases and lace table runners. She sewed us dresses and never took pay. When our fathers remarried, we missed Marian Lewis.

Katie said in the car, "I always thought of Marian as more of a mother than Sarah ever was. Did you think of Bethna as a mother to you?"

Like cows heading home, we go down the same trails when we talk about Cottertown. "Bethna," I said, "was good to me."

I always say that. And Katie says next, "Oh, Sarah was good, but she had her own children."

I noticed all at once that the fog had come back.

"I see it," said Katie, "but we're practically home."

"We still have the bridge." And deer in the road and no telling what.

"Don't worry," she said. That's Katie all over, charging ahead. "What I wish I knew is if Marian Lewis was really kin to that man." A man who stayed over a few times a month, a hardware salesman she called Cousin Bill. "I bet you a dime they were sleeping together."

Of course they were. We both know that, but as children we didn't, and the children inside us won't rest without proof.

"That was nervy, you know, with two girls upstairs. We might have come down."

"We never did that."

"To get water or something."

I saw up ahead a face in the fog. A woman I knew. I wasn't sure who. "Stop!" I said.

Katie slammed on the brakes. "My God, it's the bridge."

It *was* the bridge. Not a woman at all, but the eerie rearing of the rusty old arch, without feet in the fog and no sign of railing or roadway either. As blind as moles we had run up on it.

"We might have gone off!" Katie exclaimed.

Shaken, I said, "I saw something else."

"It's the bridge," she repeated, and rolled down her window. "Do you hear a car coming?"

I rolled down mine. "I don't hear a thing." A warm breeze was blowing. The wind had shifted and the air was like spring. Spring in December when two days ago we were freezing to death.

"This is awful," said Katie. "I can't drive across if I can't see the railing." She poked out her head. "I could back up, I guess, and park on the shoulder."

"There's no shoulder here. It falls off to the creek as it nears the bridge." I opened my door. "I'd better get out."

Katie grabbed my coat. "Don't you dare get out!"

I wouldn't have usually—for any amount—but I had the odd feeling I'd be safe on the bridge. "I'll just have a look."

"What could you see?" She held on tightly till I settled back in.

"Okay. You're the boss."

She said in a wail, "I am not the boss!"

"We have to decide what we're going to do."

"You hurt me, Sibby, calling me boss."

I've done it before and she never objected. "I'm sorry," I said. "But we can't stay here. If a car comes along..."

We sat still and listened. It seemed to us both that far down the road a car was approaching.

"Let's hurry," I said.

"Hurry? How? Where do I go?"

"Steer straight ahead."

"It's too dangerous, Sibby!"

My course seemed clear. "I'm going to get out and walk next to the headlight. Steer to the right. When I touch the railing, I'll signal," I said.

"Are you crazy?" said Katie. She remembered, I'm sure, what a coward I am. But I felt very strong and sure of my plan.

"I can do this," I said. "If a car does come, it will have room to pass."

"An inch," Katie said. I could tell she was crying.

Was I crying too? Up on the bridge my face was so wet from the fog blowing on it I couldn't distinguish tears from the mist. I didn't care to, really—or think of it, even. I had to be careful not to step where the planks weren't. "You'll break your fool leg," I said to myself.

I motioned to Katie to start the car rolling. *If Bob could see this,* was what I was thinking. Out in the fog it was hard to breathe. With my hand on the headlight pointing the way, I felt as I used to as a child in the movies when I covered the aisle light and looked at my bones glowing orange in my flesh.

Slower! I signaled. I wished I had told her to honk if the car came, to sit down on the horn so they'd know we were there. But at least I had flats on instead of high heels.

The railing emerged, wet and cold at my side. "Straighten out!" I yelled.

Katie put out her head. "I can't understand you."

In a minute she got it, and we started again. I could see the car coming. In my mind I could see it, moving ever so slowly. In time with us. *Our destiny, Katie,* I said out loud. What answered was coyotes down on the creek bank or back in the woods, yipping and howling like dogs in the pound at Marian Lewis's when we curled in our beds and covered our ears.

I was touching the railing and touching the headlight. A bridge myself. Or a spoke in a wheel.

I thought of Marian Lewis on the day of her death with her soul flying up and all of her memories leaving her brain.

"Mother," I said.

Katie tapped the horn.

"What's the matter?" I yelled.

"This is driving me *crazy!*"

"We'll be off in a minute."

"Off in the water. I'm getting out."

I screamed, I think. "Stay where you are!"

"You're safe out there, you don't care about me. I'm going to be hit."

"Don't get out of the car!"

"Let the damned car go. I want to be saved!"

We heard the other car coming, its engine noises, its tires grating gravel, still a way off, but steadily coming.

"Oh God, oh Sibby, we're going to be killed!"

"Listen, Katie. Stay in the car and keep driving slowly. Do you hear me, Katie?"

She did what I said.

In a few minutes' time I was sitting beside her. We were off the bridge, on the gravel ourselves, still feeling our way, but not in danger of diving. The worst we could do was crash in the ditch.

"Can we stop now?" said Katie.

"We'd be hit from the rear."

"There's nothing to hit us. There's no one out here, no one but us."

I thought she was right, but I wasn't sure. "We both heard a car."

"We don't hear it now." We stopped breathing to listen. "It must have turned off."

"Then stop if you want to."

She kept going on. "I've been thinking of Bob, what a fit he'll have. Are you going to tell him you got out on the bridge?"

"Not for a while. Maybe never."

"That's wise," Katie said. "We're safe and sound so what does it matter?"

"We're not out of the fog."

"It's thinning," she said.

I saw she was right. Away from the water the fog bank had dwindled to wisps in the headlights and drops on the windshield of make-believe rain.

"Were you frightened?" asked Katie.

"Scared to death. At one point," I told her, "my lips stuck together."

"Ha," Katie laughed. "Too scared to spit. I've heard about that."

"You weren't scared, of course."

"I went all to pieces."

"You did what I told you."

"I had to," she said. "When I tried to get out, the seat belt held me."

"You could have undone it."

"I couldn't think how."

On the outskirts of town Katie patted my knee. "You were brave to get out."

"I was led," I said. "I was given a sign."

"A sign?" she exclaimed. "What do you mean?"

"A face in the fog. My mother's, I think. Or it could have been Marian's."

"You imagined it, Sibby."

"Maybe," I said. "But we stopped just the same."

"Is that why you stopped us?"

"It's all right, Katie. It's all over now."

"We could have run off in the water. We would have been killed!"

"Too absurd," I said. Bob would say that. "The two daughters of women who died the same day?"

"It could happen," said Katie.

"One chance in ten million. In twenty-five million, coming back from the funeral of the woman who sheltered us after they died."

We rode down the street where both of us live.

"Sibby," said Katie, "I must tell you something."

This is it, I thought. The thing that waits in the lives of us all. "Go ahead and tell me."

"The day of the picnic I was the cause of the lemonade spilling."

"You weren't," I said—when I had words to say it.

"I was," she insisted. "I was reaching across for another sandwich."

"I knocked it over. Swatting a fly."

Katie stopped at my house. "We didn't both do it."

"I did it," I said. "I've always known it."

"Why didn't you tell me?"

"You didn't tell me."

We had a big cry right there in the street. When I blew my nose I saw Bob looking out with the lights behind him. "I have to go."

"Thank you, Sibby."

"Thank you for the ride."

Katie drove off. I moved on, too, toward the house and Bob, past the ghosts of old bedspreads asleep on the lawn.

Strangers and Pilgrims

ESTHER was eating chips for her lunch, licking salt off her fingers while the TV repeated *Rain through this evening, rain ending in snow.*

"Snow," she scoffed. She was still in her nightgown and battered old slippers. "It won't snow in Houston."

Then the telephone rang.

She had to step over things before she could reach it. The place was a mess. Kleenex in balls all over the floor. Dishes stacked, the bed in a snarl. The voice on the line said, "Esther? It's Nola."

Nola who? She stared at the sofa. *Nola McMillan.* Nola was calling! "Where are you?" she asked.

"I'm down at the bus station."

"The bus station here?"

"Can you come and get me?"

After thirty-four years and not even a postcard?

"Esther?"

"Oh. Oh, I don't know. I've been sick with a cold."

"Esther, come on!" She heard Nola's laugh.

"You have a car, don't you?"

"I have my mother's green Chevy."

Nola said quickly, "Is Aunt Ruby dead?"

"She died last summer."

"Oh, Esther. I'm sorry. I loved Aunt Ruby."

"She wasn't really your aunt."

"She was Uncle Mac's sister."

"Stepsister," said Esther. Nola groaned. "She wasn't your aunt, but she took up for you. After your downfall."

A pause on the line. "Is that what you called it?"

"It's one thing I called it." Esther saw Nola now. Saw her plainly, one hand on the phone box, her face ducked down. Smoking, of course. Dressed in something outrageous, tiger skin shoes or something else silly.

"Well, are you coming? Or shall I hang up?"

"It'll be a few minutes. I have to get dressed." Esther put down the phone. *Nola,* she thought. *If I'd gone out for bread I could have missed her entirely.*

Uncle Mac came with the news when the girls were both eight. He was a big handsome man who soon would be dead, but he wasn't dead then. He was Arthur McMillan, running his cleaning shop, Mac's-on-the-Corner, and living on Harwood, the best street in Willit.

"Nola's homeless," he said to Esther's mother. "Her daddy's off the track again in Jefferson Parish and her mother's mixed up with somebody else. The child's out in the cold, so Faustine and I, we're bringing her here, to live with us."

Faustine, Mac's wife, was afraid of children. "What do they eat?" she asked Esther's mother.

"Doughnuts," said Esther, who was lying down, having one. "And fried chicken breasts and hot rolls with butter."

Nola hadn't arrived yet, only the letter from Virgie, her mother. "On lavender notepaper," Faustine said to Ruby. "It smelled up the mailbox with toilet water."

"What kind of water?" Esther asked, but nobody answered because Faustine was crying.

"With a child to look after, when will I practice?" Faustine played the violin. She played in concerts all over the country. She wore mascara makeup when most women didn't, and orange Tangee on her brownish lips.

"Ruby," begged Mac, "can't you calm her down?"

Ruby, his stepsister, went on mending. She was a smooth-browed woman who let nothing upset her that was not on the radio. When Hubert went off, she was left with Esther, not quite two, and two quarts of motor oil nobody wanted.

"Damn Hubert's hide!" Mac had raged. "How's Ruby going to live?"

Ruby got along. She did ironing for people and cooked for their parties.

She baked little square nut cakes with delicious green icing. They were Irish, she said. The secret ingredient, she let get around, was oil of shamrock. Those lucky green cakes paid the bills till Pearl Harbor. Then she worked in munitions with a snood on her head.

"Why is Nola coming?" Esther wanted to know when the Macs had gone. "Did her father die? Is she really my cousin?"

"Nobody has died." Ruby snipped a thread. "Clinton and Virgie are separated. Like your father and I." Like the whites and the yolks that fluffed up the cakes. Esther thought of her stomach: a little cafe where cake sat in the cake booth, and ham and peas in the next two beside it. A dim light burned there the size of an orange. "Will I like her?" she asked.

"Nola? Of course. She'll be a nice little playmate." Ruby twisted the dial of the Atwater-Kent. "Now nothing else, please. Here's *Stella Dallas*."

The day Nola arrived, she came up the sidewalk between Mac and Faustine wearing canvas sandals and a pink-striped sunsuit still creased from the store.

"She's all head," Esther said.

"Shh-h," said Ruby. "It's because of her curls."

They ate slices of watermelon out on the lawn. Nola named every seed she took from her mouth. Two slippery white ones she called Ben and The Baby.

"Who?" Esther asked and spit hers at the cat.

While Nola unpacked in the house on Harwood, Esther watched from the bed. "Do you think you'll stay?"

"I'll stay if I want to." There were scabs on her knees where she'd fallen in gravel. Or was pushed, Esther thought.

"What is that scar from?" A bright purple snake that ran down her neck.

"I had poisoned blood and they drained it there."

"A doctor or who?" Esther leaned over closer. "I know why you're here. Because Clinton's in jail."

Nola gave her a shove. "You mind your own beeswax, you elephant's butt!"

"Damn you!" cried Esther, flat on the floor.

Faustine must have heard, but she didn't come in. She closed a door softly and turned on the Bendix.

Nola's hair had turned gray. Esther couldn't get over it. "You can dye it, you know."

"Maybe I will." Nola tapped off her ashes in the palm of her hand. Esther's car tray was full, of pennies and such.

"You look older gray."

"I am older, Esther. So are you." They were going toward Willit, for whatever reason (because Nola had asked to, to see the old house), over bumpy patched roads, off through the country where blackbirds were flying. Nola wasn't concerned. She still had her smile and the one lifted eyebrow. Nola McMillan.

"Nola Reese," she had said.

"You're married?" asked Esther.

"It didn't work out."

When she came from the bus station she carried a bag, a bunged-up brown one that went with her shoes. She wore a cloth coat flung over her shoulders, and a scarf at her throat where the scar had faded and puckered a little.

"Where have you lived?" (While they waited for gas.)

"All over," said Nola. "In Maine last year."

"*Maine,*" said Esther.

"It's not the end of the world."

To Esther it was. Texarkana was. "I've moved twice in my life. From Willit to Houston. Then to the apartment I'm living in now."

"Damn!" Nola laughed. "I believe you're proud of it."

Esther paid the man, using Nola's money, a ten-dollar bill. She drove out of the city before she said, "You were always a cusser. I never heard *shit* until you came and said it."

"I was ahead of my time." Nola stared out the window. "Hey, look at the Brahmas." White cows with humps gazed over the fences.

"*Shit Marie* was your favorite expression."

"You said *damn* the first time I met you."

"That was Uncle Mac's word. I learned it from him."

"Poor Uncle Mac."

"Poor Aunt Faustine. You don't know how she died."

"I do know. Her lawyer wrote me when he sold the house."

* * *

They drove into Willit and got out of the car as a downpour ended. Nola stood on the sidewalk and gazed at the house, a two-story brick with stoops by the steps and a wide sloping yard leading down to the street.

"250 Harwood. Look at it, Esther."

"It's the same old place." Nola made Esther tired, showing up now in the middle of February when the leaves were all down and people had colds. "Aren't we going to go in?"

"We can't," Nola told her. "It's not Uncle Mac's now."

"We can ring the bell and see what they say." Esther had on her slicker—the yellow hood zipped around—and her high school galoshes (which Nola thought should be in a museum).

"What will *you* say?" she asked Esther.

"The first thing I think of."

"As always," said Nola. Her skin was still pale. Flour sack white, Esther once noted, starting a fight that Nola had finished by biting down hard on Esther's left nipple. *My god, are these teeth marks?* Ruby had exclaimed.

"When they open the door, I'll say that you lived there during the war."

Nola turned toward the car. "I don't want to go in."

"Then why did we drive all the way out here?" Fifty-nine miles from Houston to Willit. On Nola's gas, but nevertheless.

"We can leave if you like." Nola walked off, but she kept looking back. If someone was watching, what would they think? That's what Esther thought. She was supposed to be at home getting well from her cold, and she was out in the weather, getting sicker probably.

Nola never seemed grateful to Mac and Faustine for taking her in. She wrote nasty words in the Methodist hymnals. She slipped out at night and went riding with boys. She showed them her breasts, somebody said.

"She's no kin to me," Esther announced.

"She is," said her friend, Rosemary Garnish. "Arthur McMillan is your mother's brother."

"Stepbrother," said Esther. She took pains to explain. "When their parents got married they each had children, from being married before."

"That's a sin," said Rosemary. "Married once, then getting married again."

"Only Baptists think that."

"That's what God thinks, Esther."

Nola smoked in the choir room and wore black brassieres. She inked hearts on her forehead with her Eversharp pen and placed long distance calls to Tyrone Power. One Saturday night at the picture show she wore a fake gardenia stuck in her bosom. It glowed in the dark, like an usher's flashlight.

"But it isn't red," a boy pointed out.

"What do you mean?" Esther asked.

"Would you know what I meant if I said it was green?"

He was Cabot DuPlantis, two years older, already graduated, going to college.

*   *   *

"We grew up in this place," Nola said. They were further down Harwood, where the sewer once burst and Nola's dog had dived in and splattered the fence posts.

"You practically lived on milk of magnesia."

"And prunes," Nola brooded, "and hot lemon water first thing every morning."

"Aunt Faustine didn't know what to do with you."

"She didn't know anything except playing the violin and brushing her hair."

"She had beautiful hair. She was pretty," said Esther.

"Oh sure, she was pretty." A sideways glance. "It's too bad, isn't it, her niece was so ugly."

"I'd have said you were plain," Esther replied.

"You were the niece with the duck walk and braces!"

Esther turned down a street oaks grew in the middle of. "I was better developed than you ever were. That's why you bit me."

"I bit you," said Nola, "because you were mean. You proved it, too, when you wrote that damned letter."

Esther pulled in her breath. "The intent of that letter was kindness, Nola. When you came back from New Orleans you knew where you stood."

"Shit," Nola said. "Shit Marie."

"I wrote it, Nola, in a state of shock!"

"In a state of self-righteousness, that's what you mean. Oh hell, forget it." She rolled down her window and flipped a cigarette out in the rain. "This crazy old street. Trees in the middle for drunks to run into."

"The trees are historical," Esther said. *The letter too.* History now. As easy as that, when for years she had worried, had quarreled with her mother and made herself sick for the damage she'd done, and now here was Nola, not caring a bit. "Would you like to get out and look at the markers?"

"No, I would not." Nola poked her head out and sniffed the air. "What do I smell?"

"The cotton mill probably."

"It's chocolate, that's what! It's a hot fudge sundae from Izzy's Confectionery."

"It isn't, Nola. Izzy's is gone."

"Turn at the corner."

The place wasn't there, as Esther had said and said again as she slowed the car by the space at the curb where they used to be served, a tray brought out and hooked to the door. The store beyond was something else now. The sign said BIRDS, Baby birds inside.

"What's happened to Izzy?" Nola wailed.

"He died," Esther said. "Do you want to stop?"

Nola burst into tears. "Do you want a bird?"

They drove over to Main, Nola sniffling. She took out a tissue and blew her nose. "God, I hate time. I hate what it does to us."

"Everything changes," Esther said.

"Not Linkletter-Heisig." Nola leaned out toward a thin blackish building that had come into view. "God, Esther. The Saturday afternoons we spent in that place." Wartime Saturdays, folding bandages. "Our hair tied up in those tacky scarves and those ladies in nurse caps constantly scolding. *Girls. Girls! Take off your nail polish! Wash your hands!*"

"One speck of dirt could have caused gangrene."

"The worst dirt in those days was gossip," said Nola.

Esther said quickly, "Remember those toilets? How they never would flush?"

"I remember the stairs. You always had cramps and folded up on the landings."

"But I never went home. I stayed on and worked."

"Scared you would miss something."

"I stayed," Esther said, "for the boys overseas."

"The boys and the men," Nola said sadly.

Arthur McMillan died over there. His first day in Sicily he stepped on a mine. His things were sent home: a green fountain pen, a packet of letters. Faustine wrote on the stone she covered them with: *Arthur McMillan, Murdered in Italy.*

At Easter vacation their last year in school, word leaked out at Linkletter-Heisig that Nola had *done it.* Cabot DuPlantis was who it was with. And it wasn't just once, it was over and over.

"How do you know?" Esther asked.

"Everyone knows," said Rosemary Garnish.

"The boys are telling it," Imogene added.

Nola herself was off in New Orleans, her first trip back, visiting her mother (and Ben and the baby, going on nine).

"They're lying," said Esther.

"Esther, they aren't."

The ladies in nurse caps were off at their table, removing gauze threads the girls folded in, smoothing out wrinkles, squaring corners.

"The first thing to do," Rosemary said, "is to make clear to Nola she's out of our crowd."

"Why is she out?" Esther asked.

"We can't run around with a girl who does that."

"Dirt rubs off," Imogene said.

"One bad apple can ruin a barrel." (Or a bouquet, in this case, of lily-white girls.)

"Well, how can we tell her? She's not even here."

"We'll write her a letter. You're her cousin. You'll know what to say."

"I am not her cousin!"

"I'll help you, Esther," Imogene offered.

They read it out loud after they finished. One girl wouldn't sign it. Christine LaCrosse. *When you come back to Willit, we will not be your friends.* She threw it down in the mud. They had to copy it over.

"Sign or you're out," threatened Rosemary Garnish.

"You stupid prick. I'm already out."

"Prick?" Esther asked. She looked it up in an old Funk & Wagnall, but Rosemary Garnish knew what it meant.

"Christine LaCrosse is doing it too."

Ruby (Esther's mother) said in the parlor at 250 Harwood after Mac was killed, after Nola had left, "Are you eating at all?"

"Of course," said Faustine.

Ruby snooped around (through a long strain of Haydn). "If you go on like this, you'll make yourself sick."

She no longer dressed, Ruby observed. After Nola's departure, she stopped buying groceries. She ate small easy things she got out of jars: olives and mushrooms and dark little capers.

She practiced all day. She got up at night, the neighbors said. In the dark with her bow she played Wagner, Sibelius. *Voces Intimae* all by herself.

"This omelet is good," Nola said.

"Of course it's good. I used herbs," Esther told her, "and sprinkled on sherry. I know how to cook. My mother made cakes."

"I know she made cakes."

They had quarreled in the car coming home from Willit and then come up the steps to Esther's apartment, three messy rooms they could see from the stairs. The pine dresser and wardrobe, Nola remembered—and a mug in the bathroom with swans painted on it.

"She made fluffy brown nut cakes with oil of shamrock."

"It was mint," Esther said. "It grew wild in the alley."

Nola crumpled her napkin, a thin paper thing. "Aunt Ruby looked Irish, do you realize that?"

"She was Polish," said Esther.

Nola laughed.

"She could have been Polish!" Esther went to the sink and filled it with water.

Nola stayed at the table and blew smoke through her nose. "What do you do about making a living?"

"I work," Esther said. "That's a queer thing to ask."

"What kind of work?"

"I keep books for a creamery."

"Do they still have those?"

"Don't they still have cows?" Esther turned to look at her. "What do you do?"

"Whatever I have to." Nola jabbed out her cigarette and walked to the sink. "Do you hear from Hubert?"

"Hubert who?"

"Your father, dear."

"Do you hear from your mother?"

"She's dead," Nola said.

On the way out of Willit Nola said, "That's that, I suppose."

"Meaning what?" Esther said. She had run up a fever showing Nola around.

"I hoped there'd be answers. Something to build on for the rest of my life. Something overlooked when I lived there before."

Esther steered the car down the rain-soaked road that was gravel mostly and weeds in the ditch. "Cabot DuPlantis?" Nola's old boyfriend. "Were you looking for him?"

"I stopped looking for him before I went to New Orleans to visit my mother."

"Nobody knew that."

"Nobody asked."

"Well, it wouldn't have mattered. It was too late then, the damage was done."

"None done to you," Nola said coldly. The bright end of her cigarette burned in the dusk. "Your life went on. Mine screeched to a stop."

"You're exaggerating."

"Am I?" said Nola. "I went off for a week and when I came back I had no friends. Your kind little letter—"

"You said let's forget it!"

"You sentenced me, Esther, to six weeks in hell!"

"It was not *my* letter."

"You wrote it, didn't you? You signed your name."

"Everyone signed it!"

"Yours was the Judas mark. I want to know, Esther. Did you ever feel sorry?"

Esther ran off the road and clipped a few weeds getting back on the gravel. "You did to yourself what you're blaming on me! Nobody made you have sex with that boy."

"Have *sex,*" Nola sneered. "That's the dark stuff of sin you're naming so lightly. And how do you know if he made me or not?"

"Are you calling it rape?"

"I'm calling it hormones," Nola said in disgust. "Or whatever it is that sets you on fire at seventeen."

"Why weren't the rest of us set on fire?"

"You and your friends? You were barely hatched out."

"We were all the same age."

"Chronologically maybe." Nola threw out her cigarette. "Here's the turn."

Esther swung the wheel. A splatter of gravel flew up from the tires. When the car was headed toward Houston again, she said to Nola. "You were overwhelmed? Is that your excuse?"

"I don't need an excuse. I did what I wanted. I wanted to see what all the fuss was about."

"The fuss you stirred up got us all into trouble!"

"That's something at least. But now they're all *doing it,* girls everywhere."

"And all having babies," Esther said. "It's a wonder you didn't."

"I was too smart for that."

"How did you know what not to do?"

"Faustine and Mac had their paraphernalia."

"You stole it from them?"

"Esther, my god, you still don't know what it's all about?"

"I would never have sex outside of marriage."

"I respect that, Esther, but it's all around you!"

"I don't have to notice."

Nola looked out the window where the cows had lain down. "You might have missed out."

"I don't care if I did. You get over things, Nola."

"Some things you don't." She swung back around. "Black-balling, you don't. It was terrible, Esther, what you did to me."

"There were six *other* girls …"

"But you and I, we grew up together! We were practically kin. How could you do that when you knew how I'd feel?"

"Did you care how *I'd* feel? Do you know what they said? They said *Nola's your cousin!*"

"Oh hell, what was that?" Nola was crying. "You sent the goddamned letter to me in New Orleans! They phoned Faustine! They read the thing on the phone!"

"You should have kept quiet."

"I was falling to pieces, can't you understand that? I was nothing but a *child* and I had to go back and live like a leper till graduation."

"You had Christine LaCrosse."

Nola dug in her purse for her packet of tissues. "I had Aunt Ruby or I wouldn't have made it."

"Who? My mother? What do you mean?"

"She came over to Harwood and talked to me, Esther."

"Where was I?"

"With your friends, I suppose. Off passing judgment on somebody else."

"You cried on her shoulder?"

"She offered her shoulder. Aunt Ruby was a saint, the one person I knew who showed any compassion."

"Compassion!" said Esther. "Do you know what she said when she heard about you? *I'm ashamed of you, Esther.* Ashamed of me! When you were the one who did all the bad things."

Dark shapes of trees flew by the window. "Look out!" Nola warned. "We'll land in the ditch."

"From the time I was ten she preached to me, Nola. *Don't tarnish your name with the company you keep, watch out who your friends are—*"

"Watch out for that car!"

"I could have done what you did!" Esther shouted. "After games—in the dark—in the back seats of cars! I could have had flowers stuck in my bosom, red lights and green lights— but I listened to mother—and she took up for you!"

"Listen," said Nola, "I'm going to drive."

Faustine could have toured after the war. She had offers for concerts from dozens of places. She turned them all down to be with Mac. She believed Mac was there, in another room.

"He'll come if I call." But she wouldn't disturb him. "He's absorbed in his stamps," she said to Ruby.

What could Ruby say that a telegram and Mac's green fountain pen hadn't said already? When she made up her mind she had to go live with her, Faustine locked her out. She put bars on the windows.

*   *   *

Ahead on the prairie Houston was shining.

"Did she give you the money to get out of town?"

"She did not give me money. She talked to me, Esther, that was all."

"You got it from somewhere."

"From Uncle Mac's will."

"He left money to you? Faustine was his wife. It should have been hers."

"She got all she needed to starve herself."

"Aunt Faustine died of pneumonia."

"She stopped making blood. You know that, Esther. She killed herself."

"If Uncle Mac hadn't died, she'd have been all right."

"She was never all right."

"Well, Uncle Mac loved her."

"Uncle Mac," said Nola, "loved your mother."

After the dishes, Nola dealt out a hand of solitaire and poured from a bottle she had bought at a store when they stopped for bread.

"I don't usually drink," Esther said.

"A good shot of this will break up your cold." Nola raised a shade and looked at the street, at rain falling down in sleek, lighted needles. "The times I liked best were when Faustine was touring. How old were we then?"

"Twelve," Esther said. She had changed to pajamas and a blue fuzzy robe with spots on the front, of coffee or something. "I keep the shades down. If they're down all the time, it's harder to tell if I'm up here or not."

Dramas ran through her head since she lived alone. In one she was tied up and thrown in a river (but able to swim, though she'd never learned how).

"Besides," she said, "there's nothing to see. Except Tuesdays and Thursdays when they dance over there."

The building was dark across the street. "Do you watch?" Nola asked. She wore a robe, too, and white feathered mules that showed off her ankles.

"I watch TV."

Nola played a jack on the queen of clubs. "When Faustine was away we were more like a family. Uncle Mac and I coming over from Harwood, Aunt Ruby cooking supper. Do you know what I thought when we sat at the table with our lights shining out?"

"Of course I don't know."

"I thought someone was watching out there in the dark, somebody wishing they could come in."

Esther set down her drink. "I know what it was. A greyhound," she said.

"A greyhound!" laughed Nola.

"I dreamed of it once. This dog on his hind legs in a top hat and glasses. He raced up to our door with foam on his mouth." Esther wiped her lips. "I tried locking the screen. I had my hand on the hook, but you know how it is, you can't lift your arm, you can't move your fingers."

"You were having a nightmare."

"He breathed in my face. A horrible smell. I could erp right now, just thinking about it."

Nola leaned on her chin. "I dreamed something once."

"I dream every night. You're supposed to," said Esther.

"This was last year in Maine. I was walking down Harwood. I went in our house."

"We should have done that today instead of standing there gawking like a couple of dopes."

"I went inside. And guess what I saw." Nola touched Esther's wrist. "Someone had painted everything white. *White,*" she repeated "Right down to a lizard, stuck on the wall, breathing still."

Esther looked at her hazily. "What kind of lizard?"

"One of those green ones, except it was painted. Its little white sides pumped in and pumped out. I could see its heart racing. Esther," said Nola, "the lizard was *me.* I knew just how it felt, how desperate it was."

Esther gazed at her solemnly. "Nuts," she said. She got out of her chair and went to get chips and brought them back to the table. "Dreaming a greyhound didn't make me a dog."

Nola sighed. "The dog," she said, "was a sexual symbol."

"You're hipped on sex."

"What about you? If Old Bogeyman Sex got ahold of you, he'd have himself something."

"You're drunk."

Nola smiled. "Let's drink a toast." She lifted her glass. "To Mac and Ruby. They were sweethearts, you know."

"They weren't," Esther said. She took a handful of chips and chewed them to nothing. "They were brother and sister."

"They weren't kin at all. They were nineteen years old when their parents got married—and soon after that, Mac was a father."

"A father! To who?"

"To me, for one." Nola met Esther's stare. "I thought maybe you knew."

"How would I know?"

"Aunt Ruby could have told you."

"You're making this up. Clinton wasn't your father? Was Virgie your mother?"

"Esther, of course."

Esther breathed through her mouth as if she'd been running. "Did Clinton know?"

"Virgie fooled him for years. She could have fooled him till yet if she hadn't met up with Ben and got pregnant with Baby. They had a big row and it all came out." Nola fingered the scar that coursed down her neck. "He just about killed us, my mother and me."

"This is making me sick."

"You need a fresh drink." Nola poured a thin stream into Esther's glass. "There's more to this tale."

"Well, I don't want to hear it!"

"You'd rather live your whole life in ignorance, Esther? And die after a while and not ever know that we're probably sisters?"

"Sisters!" said Esther. "We aren't even cousins!"

Nola crooked her eyebrow. "What are we then? Why am I here?"

"Because you got off the bus!" Esther swept the playing cards into a drawer and slammed it shut. "Did Aunt Faustine know Mac was your father?"

"We never discussed it. But it said in his will."

"It didn't say, did it, that *I* was his daughter?"

"Not flat out," Nola admitted. "But think how they acted. They touched all the time. And your father ran off. You know he knew."

"Nola," said Esther. She flattened her palms on the table between them. "Did anyone reasonable tell you this?"

"Not Aunt Ruby, if that's what you're asking. But I know it's the truth."

"There's no truth to it. Don't ever mention it to me again."

"Esther," said Nola, "why can't we be sisters?" Her pale hands fluttered. "There's nobody left. They've all of them died," she said on a high note. "It's just you and me, alone in the world."

"The world's full of people."

"Not people who know us, who know our past."

"With a past like yours, you ought to be glad."

"God, you're a jerk." Nola took a long breath. "You're a first-class jerk, and you don't even know it."

"I'm sorry I said that."

"You aren't," Nola said. "You're Esther, that's all, and there's no help for it."

Nola left the room. Like a queen, Esther thought. When she was eight years old she walked like a queen and bossed people around. Even Mac and Faustine—and now Mac was her father!

Esther chewed up an ice cube, and then leaned to the window to pull down the shade. "Why, it's snowing," she said.

She went shouting to Nola. "It's snowing in Houston! The street is all covered, there's snow on the cars!"

Nola sat on the toilet, creaming her face. "So it's snowing," she said.

"I guess it's nothing to you, from Maine and all, but it doesn't snow here. It hasn't snowed good since the fifties, remember?"

Nola stood up. "I was gone by then." She walked past Esther on her thin white legs and got into bed with the twisted-up sheets. "My lighter played out. Do you have any matches?"

"Of course I have matches." Esther went to the kitchen and brought back a folder. "The creamery I work for gives them away. Brandt's is the name. You can see on the cover."

She watched Nola's smoke curl toward the ceiling. "They're hiring now. You could probably get on."

"I'm not staying here. I'm going out West."

"Suit yourself, but they're good-paying jobs. You could settle down, get ahold of yourself."

"You're missing the snow."

"I'm going in a minute." Esther sat on the bed. "About that other."

"What other, Esther?"

"You asked in the car if I ever felt sorry. I am sorry, Nola. I've been sorry for years. Imogene, too. We used to sit in her swing and wish we could tell you."

"You should have written a letter."

"I'm serious, Nola. We worried for years that we might go to hell."

"You might make it yet. It's still on the books."

"It might do you good to say you forgive me."

"I forgive you, Esther."

"Say it like you mean it."

"God," said Nola. "What else do you want? Shall I call up Imogene and bawl on the phone?"

"I wish you could. But I don't know her number. I don't know where she is."

Nola closed her eyes. "I'm tired, Esther. Turn off the light."

"Don't go to sleep with that cigarette burning."

Fo Nut X

GRACKLES SWOOP IN and take over the tree, noisy black fruit on all of its branches, their sound going out like saws in the wind.

"It's spring," Josie says in her actress voice. Her socks have worked down in the heels of her shoes. In her satchel are books—five Nancy Drews—and none of her lessons which are all back at school in her untidy desk: a brown squatty animal eating hay, straw sticking out from the sides of its mouth, and straw on the floor (arithmetic papers).

"How do you know your mother is pregnant?"

"She pokes out in front, and she can't wear her clothes." Josie swings along in her skirt and her sweater, neither a match, the sweater with pudding streaks on its breast.

"Maybe she's fat."

"It's a baby," she says. "I saw them doing it."

"You saw them! When?"

"A long time ago."

"Why didn't you tell me?"

"I'm telling you now." One minute she's giggling and wetting her pants, and the next thing you know she's Bette Davis.

"If you saw them," I say, "what did you see?"

"I didn't see much."

"How much?" I insist.

I am taller and older-looking than nine. Mature, mothers say. They tell their children, "If Lanny is going, you can go too." It's a wonder, I think, that anyone likes me.

Old Mother Lanny, Josie has named me. *Because you're so big.* Josie is tiny with black quick eyes and milky-white skin. She smells of bananas. Her slips hang down. *I know what you wish. You wish you were smaller.*

"Josie," I plead. "What did they do?"

"They were rolling around." The giggles begin, both of us laughing.

"In the bed?" I say.

"Of course in the bed." We have to sit down. We sit under the tree. The birds lift off and land on the light wires.

The tree is Josie's, close to her house. An oak of some kind that startles in spring with its chartreuse leaves. In the fall it's gold. The Marker Tree. It marks where she turns in all of the seasons, where she stops and looks back, four blocks down the hill at me turning too, waving good-bye. Sometimes we shout with our arms in the air, like men do on ships with flags in their hands. Sometimes we're angry and don't look at all.

"Start over," I say. "What happened first?"

"I went to the bathroom and heard all this racket."

"The springs?"

"I guess." We snicker and snort. "I peeped in at the door and he was on top of her."

"Your father?" I say. Mr. Parnell, who works for the city. Who once climbed the roof and helped me get down. "The part I don't get is where does his thing go?"

"*Lanelle*," Josie says.

"Well, how would I know? You don't know either."

"It goes in her place."

"What place?" I say. "Does everyone have one?"

"Women," says Josie. "Men have their thing."

We fall over laughing and lie on our backs, the blue sky above us, the shaving cream clouds.

"My parents," I tell her, "would never do that."

"Especially your father." He comes in at five and goes in the kitchen. While he's fixing his highball we're supposed to stay out. "The only thing is ..."

I know what it is. My parents have children, my brothers and me. "Three times for sure," I answer her glumly.

"Can you see it?" says Josie.

"I can't," I admit. What I see is a darkness, a cloud more or less where inside it happens, then babies come out.

* * *

At night in my bed I lie the wrong way, my feet at the headboard, my head at the toe. To catch the cool breezes. If there are any breezes.

I don't lie on my back since Mr. Zucker has died.

"Why not?" says Josie.

"You know why not." She was there when we viewed him, wax blocking his nostrils.

"Mr. Zucker was dead. You're still alive."

"But how will they know?"

"Who?" she inquires.

"Whoever comes in and sees me not breathing."

"Why won't you be breathing?"

"People stop in their sleep. My Uncle Hart does."

"He's old," Josie says.

"He's nineteen!" I reply.

We scuffle and pinch and get pushed off the sidewalk. We are walking near Josie's, looking at houses. The Ghost House for one. Three stories high with the windows knocked out.

"Tramps sleep there in winter," Josie reminds me. The whole subject of tramps is one we go over. They come in on boxcars and come by in the morning and knock on the door.

When the tramps come around I don't always go out. My mother goes out and gives them their coffee.

They are men with rough beards and old winter coats.

"They look at young girls," Josie informs me.

If I'm finished with breakfast I give them their oatmeal or give them a quarter. "We don't give them work so they won't hang around and think how to rob us."

"Tramps write on the phone posts," Josie says. "They make little white chalk marks that tell other tramps which houses to go to."

We stop at the Ghost House and try to find marks. "I bet the men are inside. Drinking," I say, "and spitting tobacco."

Josie says, thrilled, "Let's go in and see!"

"I don't think we should."

But it's spring, we remember. The tramps are gone. To Florida, Dad says, to lie on the beaches.

We climb to the top and look out across town. There is wind in the house, and old yellow paper. Over the trees we can see the bay.

"Mr. Zucker was fishing when he fell over dead."

"I know that," says Josie. Mr. Zucker taught science and sports at our school. He had favorites, we thought. *Coach,* they all called him. We never did. "He had a trout on his line."

"Did they eat it?" I wonder. Or throw it back in?

"Here's a mattress!" calls Josie. "I dare you to lie on it."

"I don't take dares." I don't even look at it.

Josie inspects it. "See these brown circles? That's where they wet."

When we're out of the house, I think how it was when the windows were in it. When the cabinets had dishes; the mattress, a bed. "Who lived there?" I ask.

"Major Black and his sons. They all played the trumpet."

"Where was his wife?"

"Dead, I suppose."

"Where did they move to?"

"Watch," Josie says. She twirls in her skirt, blue with six gores. Like Deanna Durbin's.

At the end of the block we come to the house where the man killed himself. A pink stucco house that almost looks natural.

"How did he do it?" I ask again.

"He drowned in the bathtub one Saturday morning."

We have stopped here before and stared at the entrance, at the porte cochere where the body came out. "Why did he want to?"

Debts, I'd been told, but today Josie says, "His wife ran around."

To club meetings, I think. To too many bridge games and luncheons and parties. "He died just for that? He should have told her to stop it."

"She had a boyfriend, you goon."

"His wife had a boyfriend?" I have never heard that. I have heard how he drowned by lying down naked and breathing-in water. I once saw a man nude at the beach. He was changing his clothes in the cottage we rented. *Hey!* he yelled out and jumped like a jaybird without any feathers. "Who was her boyfriend?"

"Some salesman," says Josie. "Of carpets, I think."

I look at the house, the windows and doors, the cutouts in the shutters of half-moons and stars. "When it happened," I say, "did the salesman feel awful?"

"The wife was the one. She went all to pieces."

I did hear about that, how she cracked like a mirror. From grief, I supposed. But now there's more to it: a man who sold rugs, rolling on top of her.

We find out in June when the baby is coming.

"August the fourth. Edward Eugene," Josie says sadly.

"What's wrong with that? Eddie, we'll call him."

"I asked for Clark. Clark Gable Parnell."

"Ask for a girl."

"They already have one."

The Parnells buy a horse for Josie to ride. We go after school and get it out of the pasture. An old gray nag with its bones showing through.

I walk all around it. "Put on the saddle."

"The blanket goes first."

The bridle is on, the bit in its mouth. "Stand on the steps," Josie commands. "I'll bring him up close. Put your foot in the stirrup."

We are riding at last. Riding a horse. I hang onto Josie who clucks *giddy-up*. The nag, unfazed, ambles along. We are wearing straw hats tied in knots at our chins. Josie wears chaps, a gift from her uncle.

"Let's sing," she says.

We sing "Home on the Range."

"What happens," I ask, "when I want to get off?"

"You can slide down the tail."

"I'm not going to do that!"

"We'll see," Josie says.

She directs the horse with a tug on the reins. It goes off through the trees, through *bois d'arcs* with apples. Horse apples, they're called, the bright green of leaves.

We look in a nest where a bird has laid eggs.

"Let's take one," says Josie.

"I don't think we better."

"Old Mother Lanny," she says through her nose. She puts two in her pocket over her breast, a rubbery knob she says is a breast.

She fans with her hand. "It's *hot* on the trail."

"Take off your hat. I'm taking off mine." I push back my hat to bob on my shoulders. We yodel awhile as we rock along, the nag eating grass and drooling green slime.

"This is fun," Josie says.

"It is," I agree.

We talk over things—the boys we like, and how friends can be hateful.

"Two-faced," Josie says.

"Selfish," I say.

A low-hanging limb catches hold of my hat—which is tied at my throat in a never-slip knot.

"*Gah!*" I choke and clamp onto Josie.

She thinks there's a snake. "Where is it?" she screams.

"*Gah, it's my hat!*"

Josie wiggles around. "I see what's the matter. You're hung on the tree."

"Back up the horse."

"You can't back a horse."

"*Back the damn horse!*"

When finally I'm free I get the hat off and get to the ground without even thinking.

"See? It's so easy." Josie slides down. "The next time we ride—"

"The next time!" I say.

We lead the horse home and don't tell anybody. We lie in the grass where the clover is blooming.

"I was just about hung by the neck until dead."

"I saved you," says Josie.

"Last year I saved you." We went under three times in the Guadalupe River. We were wading at church camp and stepped in a hole. The others were swimming. Josie and I were rising and sinking and climbing each other like dogs in a fight. At the very last minute my foot found a ledge.

"Let's look at the eggs."

"What eggs?" Josie says.

"That you took from the nest."

She fingers her pocket. "They were crushed underfoot. By Silver," she adds.

"Silver!" I scorn.

"He once was a trick horse."

"He wasn't. You're lying."

"A girl rode him bareback."

"Josie," I say, "they would have made birds."

One thing we do when there's nothing to do is look at the writing inside my garage. Tall painted letters. FO NUT X.

Josie sits on the washbench. "What do they spell?"

"They spell NUT in the middle."

"Nut what?" she asks.

Nut X is the answer.

"But what do they mean?"

I don't know what they mean. Nobody knows, no one I've found.

"Someone took paint and just painted them there?"

"FO could be FOR with the R left off."

"For Nut?" Josie scoffs. "Maybe it's FOOD. FOOD NUT X."

"There's not enough room for that many letters."

"Well, somebody knows. Go and ask *them*." Them is my brothers who frighten her so with their cowboy boots that she hides behind doors when she hears them coming. "They started a word and forgot how to spell it."

"Okay, what's the word?"

In her movie star voice she says, "Something with Fox. I bet you that's it. FOX NUT X."

* * *

We make plans for the baby. We will take him on strolls where the horse apples grow. If he wets, we will change him. But we draw the line there.

Personally I plan to give him a dollar. And maybe blue socks. "He'll look cute in blue socks."

Clark Gable Parnell is born a month early and dies the next morning.

We cry, but not much. It doesn't seem real.

"A rosebud," weeps Josie, "that never did bloom."

"Did you see him?" I ask.

"Of course," Josie says. "He was perfectly formed."

Her mother has told her. Or Mr. Parnell. "Will they do it again?"

"I don't think they will."

We wait on the porch steps and watch for the postman. He is bringing me lipstick. A tube of Tangee. I sent off a quarter. (For a dime and a nickel I could have had lotion.)

"Let's look at the words."

We go around back. The wash is hung out. My father's white shirts are flapping their wings.

Josie sits on the washbench. "Do you really not know?"

I am trying to work out how men drown in bathtubs. And why others die with fish on their hooks.

"I've got it!" she says. "I know what it is."

"What is it?" I ask.

"A face cream we'll order. Fonuts and Exes. To take off our wrinkles."

I see it's a joke. "A vanishing cream. You vanish at night and come back in the morning."

Except babies don't.

When babies are gone, they are gone and that's it.

We cry a lot then.

When finally we're through, Josie looks at the printing in paint on the wall. "We won't ever find out."

I think this is so. But I want to keep hoping. "Maybe it's code."

"Maybe," says Josie, "tramps put it there."

Helens and Roses

THE MINUTE the job was done and the man drove away, leaving the trailer windows covered with toast-colored blinds drawn tight as Dick's hatband, Pep started complaining. "You can't hardly tell if it's daylight or dark since you put up these curtains."

"Blinds," Lula said, already feeling the difference they made. The cost, of course, had knocked her flat. But she'd long ago learned what you want in this world you have to pay for, and she wanted those blinds, more than new chairs or an air conditioner.

"What for?" Pep said when she brought up the subject the first time around.

"We need them," she said. She couldn't explain the pure-D fright of night coming on since they moved into town, of the dark reaching out from the houses and streets. From she didn't know where. "We need protection," was what she told Pep.

"What I need is air," Pep said now. "Let's raise the things up."

"We just put 'em down." Lula walked back and forth, admiring the blinds. The toast color was right. It lifted the gloom of the mud-colored walls and made the rooms airy. "Stretch out on the couch if your head is hurting."

"What hurts is to think what that bozo charged."

"No more than they're worth. They dress up the place."

"Your teacups do that—and they don't stop the breeze."

The first time the man came, he came on a Thursday, one of Pep's bad days. He brought his dog. Then he started right in with how hot it was, how he'd have to step out and see about Sheri out in the van.

"Scheherezade," Lula said to Pep, back in the bedroom where he'd gone to lie down. "That's the name of the dog."

"There's a dog in the house?" His blue eyes opened. Pep missed Prince Rudy, the best hound of his life that he'd had to sell off on account of the rule Lula had made, *No dogs in town,* when they moved from the Sandies. *They can't run loose, and they sure as the dickens aren't coming inside.*

"She's out in the van," Lula said. "Sheri, he calls her."

"Who? His wife? Why don't she come in?" Pep got off the track when his head acted up. Sometimes just a minute. Or maybe all day, the way it was lately.

As a general rule, though, they did pretty well. They lived clean lives, Pep liked to say, and except for his mix-ups, his mind stayed clear. Clearer than hers, Lula claimed. He could tell you dates way back to the Flood, even days of the week when certain things happened, especially his dog deals, like trading the setter in '38 to Pinky McClure for a broad-nosed sow and a couple of shoats. (On a Tuesday that happened—a May afternoon right after a shower.)

"Lie there and rest," Lula said that Thursday. "When he comes back here, you can move to the front."

Lula herself had varicose veins. And hemorrhoids at night. Let her turn on her back and they started in throbbing. She had learned a trick, though—to bear down for a minute, not too hard—and the pain went away. That's all there was to it, a few minutes of pressure. Gravity, she guessed it was. Out of the blue, she knew how to do it.

"What's he coming back here for?"

"To measure the windows."

"Why?" Pep said.

"For the blinds. I told you."

The next time the man came he brought the blinds with him. He left the dog in the yard, tied to a tree. She ran all around it, yipping and yapping.

"She's a nervous animal," Lula said.

"Yes, ma'am," said the man. "Spoiled rotten." He looked spoiled himself, Lula thought. He had a loose kind of look around his mouth and watery eyes set close to his nose. "She belongs to my wife, but my wife's with our daughter. In Panama City."

"Where the dictator is?"

"In Florida, ma'am. How is your husband?"

"He's all right today. He'll be out in a minute."

The man stood on a footstool. "It's the heat, I suppose, that gives him those headaches."

"Pep's ninety, you know."

"He sure doesn't look it."

"I'm eighty-five."

"You don't look it either."

Pep said again, "Let's put up those shades."

"It's nighttime, Dad."

Dad was only a name. They never had children. Never wanted them much, Pep had told his brother, which wasn't the truth. They hoped for two. Pep wanted twins. They had to fill up their lives in place of those children. Pep took up dogs. Lula settled on teacups and various things.

They were younger, of course, up on the Sandies, a little dry creek that could rise when it wanted but mostly ran quiet, bedded in sand with a few brown pools that a fish or two slept in.

They were there fifty years. Then they moved into town.

Their trailer just fit on a sliver of land next to the Quik-Stop, down a little, with a hedge in between, but the lights from the cars swept in at all hours, giving Lula the jitters.

"Like spotlights," she said. "Like they're hunting us down." She mentioned the blinds.

Pep voted for shades. "They come a lot cheaper."

"With blinds," Lula said, "you can tilt in the light and still have your privacy."

The day the man hung them he gave her some tips about which way to turn them.

"Most people get it backwards. They turn the slats down." He was sweating by then. "But let's say, for example, there's a peeper outside."

It gave Lula a chill to think that there might be.

"With the slats tilted down they look like they're closed, but out where he's at, he gets the whole picture."

He sent Lula outside to prove he was right.

She told this to Pep, helping him dress. "He sure knows his business."

Pep wound his watch. "Has he brought in the dog?"

"He brought her up the steps and gave her some water. She's roped to the tree, a little fluffy orange pooch." Lula hunted her glasses, first on the dresser and then in the bathroom.

"You're wearing the things," Pep pointed out.

"For goodness sakes." Lula pushed up the nosepiece. "She's an apricot poodle."

"I know what she is. I can't think what he calls her."

"Scheherezade."

"Spell it," said Pep. He was hell on spelling. He once won a meet and was given a ribbon. *Champeen*, it said. Lula laughed when he showed her. A spelling prize and they spelled it wrong.

It starts with an *s* that's all I know." But then she went on. "It's the name of that woman who kept telling stories to stay alive. In *Arabian Nights*."

"A picture show?"

"A book when I read it. I had it in school."

School for Lula was out on the prairie. White Hall it was called. The teacher there was Miss Mabel Barnes, on her way up as an educator. She made it, in fact, to County Superintendent, and on from there right into Houston. At White Hall her mission was to introduce culture. "There are children out here that don't know a fairy tale from Adam's off ox." She was a little pale woman, born to a doctor that lived in Fort Worth when there weren't many such—female doctors.

Lula took to culture, the myths most especially, how things got like they were, why spiders make webs, that kind of thing.

Education stays with you, is what Lula said.

Viewing the blinds, she said to Pep, "I feel a lot safer."

"Safer from what?" Up on the Sandies she was scareder of june bugs than she was of the wolves. Moths gave her a tizzy, the big hairy kind that flew in the window.

Pep, however, liked all things in nature. He liked to lie in the bed with the wind on his face and listen to owls. He had talked to a fellow over at the Quik-Stop that didn't even know owls made a whooping sound. "Like a cowboy yelling *yippy-ti-yo*."

"Owls hoot," the man said.

"Well, sure they do." Pep followed him out and poked his head in the car. "But they have a cry, too."

The man drove away. "Damn city fool," Pep said to Lula.

"Safe from criminals," Lula said.

Pep snorted at that. "Do you think you'll get murdered in this sleepy burg?" He had visited great cities. He once went to sea.

"It happens all over." In Lula's nightmares, crooks knocked down the door.

It wasn't much of a door, they both agreed. When they first came to town to size up the trailer—a sleek cream and beige with a bowed-out front where Pep stretched the flag— he put into words what was holding him back. "It's too smooth inside."

It was, Lula saw. A toy kind of outfit. When you knocked on a wall it didn't sound solid. It sounded, Pep said, like a cereal box.

They bought it anyway, with most of their capital. They were too old for loans is what it boiled down to. And too old for the country. What if one of them died?

When Lula met Pep she was barely fourteen. She had her hair in a net, no shoes on her feet, and was cleaning a skillet from fish she had fried that had stuck like glue. She was out by the barn and he came riding up on a no-count horse.

He was looking for cows. This was up on the Sandies where later they settled. There was brush all around with cow paths through it and lots of wild roses in hedges so thick you could bleed to death if you hung up in one and tried in a hurry to get yourself loose.

He came out of the yaupon, all dressed up on that pitiful pony, his legs hanging down almost to the ground.

"Nice morning," he said and tipped his hat.

She knew who he was from the dent in his chin and his sky-colored eyes. Her sister had told her. "You're Pepper McLeod."

He inclined his gaze to her feet in the dust. "You're the Bennett girl with the beautiful toes."

She covered them up under chicken-scratched earth. "What are you doing way off over here?"

"They told me in town to hurry on out before you got married."

"Aw, git on." But she half-believed he meant what he said.

He got off his horse. "Let me have that skillet." He went to the trough and dipped it in. "Now give me that rag."

He hung around for a while. He asked her age. She told him sixteen and changed the subject. "Do you always go riding in Sunday clothes?"

"When I'm out meeting girls."

She guessed that was true. He had girls all over, her sister said.

Then the cows came along, mooing and lowing, and gathered around him. "Here the girls are now."

She couldn't help laughing. He got back on his horse, laughing too. "Do you ever go dancing?"

"Of course," she lied. "When I want to, I do."

"How often is that?"

"When you see me you'll know."

He lifted his hat and gave her the look her sister had told her made girls pitch over and faint in the road. "Good-bye, Lula Bennett."

She loved him already. "Good-bye, Pep McLeod."

He didn't come back. He forgot her, she guessed.

In the time he was gone she got a lot older. She broke her wrist cranking a car. She bobbed her hair, got thin in the waist, bought a pair of kid gloves, and spent her money on dresses instead of the church.

She was working by then on a telephone switchboard and going out with men who bragged on her looks and asked her to marry them. One owned a saloon and a domino parlor and drove a Ford car the top went down on. Emmit Steele he was named, for his father the barber. He bought her a ring, but she wouldn't wear it. She said maybe she might if the sign got right.

Her sister got married. Her father died. Her mother moved off from the place on the Sandies.

Lula went there one day and found a black snake asleep in a chair. In the room that was hers, birds lay on their backs with their feet in the air.

Emmit Steele was along. "Let's get out of here."

"Wait," Lula said. She went to the window and looked at the horse trough where Pepper McLeod had scrubbed her skillet. She made up her mind. If he didn't come back she would never get married. She would stay an old maid and have put on her tombstone *Born and Died* and not a thing else.

* * *

While the man hung the blinds Lula went to the store. Not to the Quik-Stop. She went in the car. First she took off the bedspread she covered it with to keep off the cats. Then she backed it slowly into the street.

Pep said to the man. "You could bring in your dog and let her cool off."

"She's fine outside." His name was Winkle.

"These delicate dogs keel over and die."

Winkle peered toward the yard.

"Go on with your work. I'll go out and fetch her."

Lula browsed in the store. When Pep was along she had to shop fast. He bought the wrong things. He bought everything big, the biggest bananas, big boxes of crackers that always went stale.

He was married before. Briefly, to women named Helen and Rose. One was a teacher who died right away, and the other one, Rose, fell out of love.

Lula didn't know that when Pep came back. He took her out a few times and then he said, "The day Helen died—"

"Helen who?" she asked.

About Rose he said, "We married for fun."

She took it slow after that. She went out again with Emmit Steele, and a new butcher in town who sang in the choir.

Pep seemed not to mind. He met her one day by the bank on the corner. "Whenever you're ready, say the word."

She was wearing new shoes with buckles that glittered. "Ready for what?"

"To be my wife."

"Wife Number Three?"

"We'll do all right. We'll make a good pair."

"Hah," she said, "you don't respect women."

"I do." He was hurt. "I have sisters," he said.

Pep sat on the couch and drew Winkle out. "What else have you done besides hanging blinds?" He fed Sheri a cookie, a gingersnap.

"I've raced horses," said Winkle, pleased to be asked.

"My business is dogs. What'll you take for Scheherezade?"

"Oh," Winkle said, "she's not for sale. She belongs to my wife."

Pep pulled on his chin. "She's got a bum leg. You'd have to whittle your price."

"There's no way I'd sell her."

"Because of your wife." Pep studied a minute on Winkle's wife. He pictured her tall, with a downy mustache. She wore suits, he thought, and had a long neck and ears that lay back, like a panther's ears.

"Winkle," said Pep. "I'm a breeder, too. We could make us some money, depending, of course, on what ails the leg."

When Lula came home she knew right away the dog had come in. She took Pep aside.

"Sheri's been in the house."

"What makes you think so?"

"Crumbs on the rug. And I smell her perfume."

"Perfume on a dog?"

"There are people that silly."

"I'm glad I was shaving."

"You should have watched out."

When they moved into town Lula put up her teacups. Not out for display, but in boxes she stored in the two bedroom closets.

They had always sat out and Pep found he missed them, the main one especially, from Miss Mabel Barnes. A plain green cup with President Wilson in black on the side.

"The trailer's too wobbly," Lula said. "They'd fall down and break."

"What good are they doing shut up in the dark?"

"I don't want to dust them."

Pep made her sit down. "I don't think that's it."

Lula twitched in her chair. "What's the matter with you?"

He gave her the look girls had swooned in the dust for. "You gave up your cups because I can't have my dogs."

"You're the beatingest man."

"I'm right, aren't I, Lu?"

He built shelves all around and helped her unpack them. "We're fixed up now."

"All but Prince Rudy."

"Rudy," said Pep, "wouldn't like it in town."

Lula held out her arms. "Would you care to dance?"

Up on the Sandies they always went dancing. Forty miles to a dance hall was nothing at all. Except once for six weeks when Pep had pleurisy. It hurt even to walk. "It sears my chest."

He was something to scare you, a big strong man and he couldn't get up. Lula hovered around. "You ought to get out. You ought to breathe in some Vicks."

"That'd sure enough kill me." He expected to die and made plans for Lula. "You could get you a job in a cafe or something."

"I'd work on a switchboard," she said, insulted.

"They've gone out of style."

"Who says so?" said Lula.

"They've gone to the dial."

She sat down and cried for all she had lost, for marrying Pep who was sick all the time, and a barren womb, and the holes in her stockings.

"Come here, little girl."

She wouldn't go near him. "Get up from the bed! And don't talk of dying."

He talked about girls. There were more than she knew of, scattered around. Even some overseas. Alice in England. And Fleurette and Marie. He forgot where they came from. "Two really nice girls."

Lula threw the green cup and gave President Wilson a crack in his glasses. Patching him up with flour-paste glue, Pep commented mildly, "It's you that I married."

"The third on the list." She was sobbing still.

"You would have been first if you'd been a day older."

Pep went to sea in the *Tarkington Trader*. A saber ship is what it was called, for the way it cut water.

It happened right funny how he got on.

He was wasting his life, his father said—a serious man who owned two ranches and had other sons that tended to business. This one he saw as a ne'er-do-well.

"What'll it take to straighten you out?"

Pep knew right away. "Five hundred dollars." He wanted a car to drive people around, land men he'd met who came in on trains from Northern cities and couldn't get out to look at the prairies.

His father thought girls was what he was after. "You won't get it from me. Get out and earn it."

"Two-fifty?" tried Pep. He'd saved ninety himself. For two-forty more he could buy a Tin Lizzie.

"Not twenty-five cents," his father said.

He tried Mexico first and liked it fine, except for warm goat's milk and breakfast menudo—and the way they slit throats over practically nothing. He got out fast one night in September and went up to Corpus and hid on a ship.

"The damned thing sailed." He laughed, telling Lula.

She remembered those days when she had waited, forgotten. "You were gone a long time."

"Four years on the sea."

"And two wives later."

Helen died in a dentist's chair, having a tooth pulled. About Rose, Pep said, "Rose? She was pretty."

"Let's have some air," he insisted again.

"I'll fan you," said Lula, and took up *The Post*.

The women Pep married she dwelt on in bed. At other times, too. She had in her mind delicate Helen and beautiful Rose while she stood canning pears that came off the trees that bloomed on the Sandies like lace-adorned brides.

She herself was married in a preacher's front room, wearing navy blue and a hat on her head. Then they got in Pep's truck with a hound in the back and went up on the creek and settled in.

"I know about pain, Pep. I know how to stop it."

"It's not pain exactly."

"What is it then?"

He never could tell her. "Like a fog," he explained. "Like a bag on my head. Like I don't know my name."

"You bear down," Lula said. "In a minute, it's gone."

"Bear down on my head?"

"There's another way, too." She hated to tell him because it was hard, even for her (and she was all for it). "You pinpoint the pain. You search it out with a finger of thought."

"A finger of what?"

"You concentrate, Pep. You bear down with your mind on finding the pain at the place where it starts. *Is it here?* you ask. *Is this where it is?* Wherever your mind rests, the pain disappears."

"Lu," he said, "will you bring me the aspirins?"

For a living, he farmed, a handful of acres he cleared with a mule. When he had extra cash he bet on the cock fights. He made money with dogs, but they never had water that ran from a pipe, or electric power, till they moved into town.

Pep told Lula once that Emmit Steele had got rich, driving land men all over creation. "But he hasn't had fun. He hasn't had you."

"Sit up," Lula said, "and swallow these tablets." Pep gurgled them down. She thought of the day she stood at the window and vowed not to marry any man except this one. "Are you all right now?"

"Tell me a story. One of those myths."

"Scheherezade?"

"I don't care what it is."

Lula thought back to White Hall. "She married a man that was killing his wives. She had to keep telling tales till she finally saved him."

"The woman saved *him?*"

"From his murderous ways."

Pep gave a chuckle. "You tangle things up, Lu. You don't know the truth."

"Maybe I don't."

He dropped off to sleep. Then he woke up and said, "You never have known my true feelings for women."

"Hah," Lula said. "I ought to have known."

"I've been drawn to 'em somehow."

"I guess I know *that.*"

"Like a bee drawn to flowers."

"To Helens and Roses."

"Not to their bodies." He reached out and pinched her. "Except for yours. It's what makes them go, that was what pulled me."

"Eyes were what pulled you, and thick, curly hair."

"Ah, Lula, no. What I like is to watch 'em, to watch how they do. Women," he said, "are a curiosity."

Lula saw all at once that a shiver had seized him. "Are you getting too cool?" She stopped swinging *The Post.*

"No, go on."

"Go on with what?"

"Talk," he said. "It eases my head."

"Where was I?" she asked.

He couldn't quite answer. He thought he heard owls, not their cowboy cries, but the soft feathery sounds the mice probably heard and then went into trances.

"Pep?" Lula said.

He lay very still on the rim of his name and saw in the water what amounted to fish with silver-blue sides. A long time ago he had dreamed of such fish, dreamed he had caught them with only his hands.

"You're dozing," said Lula. "Pep, are you dozing?"

She watched for his breath, for the lift of his shirt or some kind of motion. "I can raise up the blind."

She pulled on the cord and the darkness rushed in with sounds from the Quik-Stop, quick feet on the pavement.

"That man let his dog in, let her up on the couch." She circled around. "That bow in her hair and her toenails painted. But I guess it's all right. She didn't have fleas." Prince Rudy had fleas. All of his ancestors leaped with fleas.

She sat down all at once and took hold of Pep's hand. "Can you see the cabin? The swing on the porch and the moon coming up with the dogs at our feet?" She started to cry then. "Remember the dancing?"

Finally she said, when the noise at the Quik-Stop had stopped altogether, "Pep, can you hear me?" She faltered a bit and then found her voice. "Up on the Sandies we never had night. We had a long spell of light." Through her eyelids she saw it, a long golden light that lasted and lasted.

Goose Girl

WHEN ROONEY'S MOTHER died, Uncle Pete Polk put her house up for sale and rented a smaller one back of the Gulf station to put Rooney in.

"This is just right for you, Rooney. You have your washroom here, we'll put your bed in there, and you can do a little cooking here in the back."

Three rooms, it sounded like, but it wasn't but two, the one bigger room and the closet-sized bathroom he was calling a washroom because that's what they called it over at the Gulf where he hung around all day and where now he would be looking at Rooney over the fence to see what she was doing when what she wanted to be doing was taking care of her geese at her house across town, with her mother well again and home from the hospital.

"I don't like it over here." Rooney was thirty-three and had positive ideas on every subject, which she was entitled to, her mother said. "She's got her own style, the same as the rest of us."

Pete called it backwardness, especially now that he was in charge of her and bent on settling her in a proper place before it dawned on her good that her mother was gone.

"There's no bathtub," said Rooney. No mirror either. Not that she cared much. She wasn't much of a dresser—pants and shirts she bought at garage sales and her hair cut short like a cap on her head. But she did like a long mirror before she went to work, in case toilet paper was stuck to her shoe or something was trailing behind her like the Kick Me signs she used to wear home from school, and one time her telephone number with a picture drawn under it that made her mother so mad she bawled out the principal.

"You put a stop to this, Junkins!" His name was Jenkins. "Those bratty kids, they're making Rooney feel dumb."

"Miss Rhoda," said Jenkins, "nobody around here is smart enough to do that."

"He's right, you know it?" Rhoda told Pete when she thought it over. "Rooney can act sometimes like a sack's been throwed over her, but then again, she sure can surprise you."

"Amen to that," her brother said. Twice Rooney had bitten him, once with her baby teeth to see how he tasted and later on when he reached for a slice of pineapple on her plate.

"I thought she was done with it!"

Rhoda bound up his hand. "She's partial to pineapple."

Rhoda spoiled Rooney, Opaline said. Opaline, Pete's wife, who had set in motion the sale of Rhoda's house and Rooney's relocation to a less valuable property. "The bungalow by the Gulf," Opaline called it. *Like it sets by the sea,* Rooney said. *More like the sewer plant,* she always added.

Spoiled or not, Rooney paid her own way. She had a long-standing job at the tailor shop and a more recent one, sitting Wednesday evenings with Grandma Polk, who wasn't right anymore and was liable to go out in the street and take off her clothes. Wednesday night was when they played Bingo over at the Hall, which Rooney liked to do, but couldn't anymore on account of Grandma Polk, who on several occasions she had prayed would die. Instead, the message got mixed up and her mother had died.

"You don't need a bathtub," Uncle Pete said. "You got this shower." He pointed it out, a pipe with a head on it, dripping through a hole in the galvanized flooring Rooney would have to stand on when she cleaned herself up.

That was the upmost important thing, her mother said. To keep yourself clean. Your body, your hair, and above all, your teeth. And always have something to wipe off your nose with.

"I don't like a shower," Rooney said. "Besides that, there's not enough room in here to swing a pig."

"You won't have to swing a pig," Pete told her. Or feed chickens either, he prevented himself from saying. He had hauled them all off—the geese too—day before yesterday when Rooney was knocked out from what the doctor gave her. When she came to herself, he said the sheriff had done it. In Rooney's best interest is what he said.

Now Rooney said to him, "If I can't swing pigs what else can I do in this squeezed-up place?"

"This nice secure house," Pete corrected. "You can watch your TV and read your books."

Rooney, somehow, was a first-class reader. Nothing else at school had impressed her much, but reading she took to. She read everything from encyclopedias to *National Enquirer*s, and every article that came out about wrestlers.

She named a dog Pete gave her after one of her favorites, Sweet Sugar Brown. His career took a nosedive when a truck hit his namesake, or so Rooney said, said so often her mother banned wrestling on TV forever.

Rooney went out and bought her own set. Two TVs going full blast on different channels was hard on the neighbors, but they had to put up with it or put up with Rooney interrupting their soap operas with a steady string of calls from the tailor shop.

"I can't read in here," Rooney told Pete. "The walls aren't painted."

"You need painted walls? Why is that, when every wall in your mama's house is bare as a baby's butt!"

"Nuh-uh," Rooney said. She fished gum from her purse and filled her mouth with it. "The dining room's painted."

"One room in fourteen, forty-five years ago."

"My bedroom's papered."

"With magazine pages."

"It's paper, ain't it?" Rooney rubbed her front teeth, a habit she had that drove Opaline crazy.

Something else worried Opaline. Rooney and men. There weren't any yet, but who knew when there would be?

"She has no restraint," Opaline said to Pete. Some of the money from the sale of the house they better set aside in case of an emergency.

"Like what?" Pete asked.

"Like having Rooney's tubes tied if things get rough."

Pete had mentioned tube-tying to Rooney's mother when Rooney came into puberty. "You need to see to it, Rhoda, before some fool boy takes advantage of her."

Rhoda ran Pete off, ran him clear to the highway. "You tend to your business and I'll tend to Rooney's!"

Now she wasn't here to do it.

It gave Pete a sour stomach, thinking what could happen if it got around town that Rooney might have money from her mother's estate. Rooney in Rhoda's house off by the highway where any kind of man could slip right in.

"I'm going to locate a truck," Pete said to Rooney, "and get you moved over here first thing in the morning."

"You're not moving me." She walked around, kicking up splinters off the floor. "I need arm room when I read. I need to be in my chair. My chair won't fit anyplace in this house."

"Don't," Pete said. "Don't start on that chair."

"It's one of a kind in the U-nited States. Just ask Father Bailey. Father Bailey said—"

"I've heard all that, Rooney."

"He said take it to a mall show, you'll get five hundred dollars!" Rooney grinned at Pete the way she did as a child when he picked her up and said, Give me some sugar. She gave him big smacks and he called her his girl.

"Do you know what, Pete?"

He seemed to be praying. "I don't want to know what."

She got up in his face with her ketone breath the doctor said she might grow out of, but never did. "I got my chair all covered with old-timey neckties. Got em at garage sales, ten cents apiece, sometimes a nickel. I got the arms and the back covered, the seat and the sides. Sewed em together without any help. It's beautiful, Pete. Did you ever see it?"

"See it, hell. Who had to go to the dump in ninety-degree weather to drag it out?"

"Wasn't me," Rooney said. "I found it, is all. On my lucky day. Just rode my bike out there and there was my chair. Finders keepers. Did you ever hear that, Pete? Finders keepers?"

"We need to move on to another topic."

"I sewed sixty-nine neckties into that cover." She showed him how, using the tail of her shirt to artificially stitch through.

"I've seen how you did it."

"You can see it again."

"Dammit, Rooney, that's the trouble with you!" A pencil-sized vein sprang up on his temple. "You talk a thing to death, you won't let it rest. You beat everything into the ground."

"Don't you holler at me!"

"You wear folks out with all your jabbering."

Rooney nailed Pete with her zebra stare. *Wild* zebra stare, Opaline called it.

They got a good look at it day before yesterday when Pete and Opaline went over to the house with buckets and sponges and cardboard boxes.

"Put everything you want in these here cartons," Pete said to Rooney, who was out in the backyard feeding lettuce to her geese. "We're putting this house up for sale. We got to get rid of things."

"You're not getting rid of any of my stuff." Rooney called her rooster. "Chick-a-chick-chick. You better come here. Better come get your breakfast."

"You come on inside now and help your Aunt Opaline."

Rooney set her hands on her hips. She had on a green nightgown and red rubber boots. "You're not the boss around here."

"I'm the executor. The executor of the estate."

Rooney picked up a bucket and poured wet chicken mash over his head.

"*Goddammit,* Rooney! Opaline! Git out here!"

His wife came running, having seen everything from the kitchen window. "I told you not to rile her! Now look what she's done. She's ruint that shirt! You ought not to wore it. I told you the blue, put the blue one on, I said."

Rooney turned a hard spray of water on Opaline.

They had to call the law, a neighbor did. When the police car rolled up, Rooney was in the henhouse gathering more eggs to throw at her aunt and uncle.

The sheriff stepped in. "Now calm down, Rooney."

She saw his badge. She flung up her nightgown to cover her face and rooted herself in the ground like a concrete piling. It took two grown men and the doctor they had to call, to drag her out. You could hear her yelling downtown before the doctor got her quiet.

It put a sweat on Pete, seeing that look again. He commenced backing off. "Now hold on, Rooney. Think what the doctor said, count to ten."

"Ten of *what?*"

"It don't matter what!"

She was swinging her purse when a sound shook the house that stopped her cold. "What the heck was that?"

"God," panted Pete, "speaking right on the money!"

"That was something blowing up!"

"A tire," he said. "Over at the station."

"A *tire!* Are you sure?"

He said, still shaken, "They blow up easy, those big old semi tires, when they're pounding the rims off."

Rooney gazed at him, thrilled. "You ever seen one?"

"Seen half a dozen."

"Wow!" Rooney said. "I wish I could see one."

"You can see em all the time when you live over here. You can get you some binoculars and see it up close."

Rooney worked her chewing gum. "Over at my house I see everything close, coons washing their feet in the chicken water. Rabbits and buzzards." She pulled on her lips. "Furthermore, I'm gonna get me a goat."

"A goat! What for?"

"The sheriff ran off my chickens. And my geese too."

"What you need is a cat. This is a nice cozy place a cat would like."

"I'd rather have a snake than a mangy old cat, always licking theirselves and coughing up hair balls. I might get me a snake. A bore constrictor. They don't have eyelids. I bet you didn't know that."

"Listen, Rooney, I'm older than you and you need to listen to what I'm telling you. That house of your mother's is way too big for a woman by herself up by the highway. You stay around there and one of these nights a hitchhiker is gonna slip in and hide in one of those rooms you don't ever use and do you some harm."

"I got locks, don't I?"

"Busters like that, they don't stop at locks."

"I bet they stop at ball bats. A hitchhiker fool with me, I'll crack his head open. I got my bat right where I sleep."

Rooney picked up her purse again, heavy as a suitcase from all she had in it, packs of letters from her pen pals all over the country, paperback books poking out the top, and a big ring of keys that didn't open anything, but came from the dump, the same as her chair.

She said over her shoulder, "I'm going home."

Pete hurried after her. "I asked you not to do that, not to go over there while we're showing the house. I asked you to stay away and you said you would."

"I changed my mind." She went down the steps and got on her bicycle. The bumper sticker on the back fender said EAT MORE RICE. The one pasted under it said JOIN THE NAVY. (She covered it up when they turned her down.)

She looked back at Pete, standing glumly on the porch. "You like this bungahole, move in it yourself."

"I can't move anywhere. I got Grandma Polk."

"And you can keep her, too, especially Wednesday nights. There's smells in that room, and noises even donkeys couldn't come close to."

Rooney rode off. She rode around a tree and came back again. "I might move in here if you get somebody to paint everything green."

"Rooney, I can't do that! I can't paint a house I don't even own."

"You're fixing to own it."

"Who told you that?" The way she gathered information was worse than a vacuum cleaner. People talking in front of her, thinking nothing would register. "You're gonna use my money to buy this house and charge me rent."

"That's a big damn lie! We would never charge you rent."

"Green," Rooney said and rode off toward town.

"There's twenty-nine hundred greens!" Pete said to Opaline.

"Send Billy Buckley over there. Let her tell him which one."

Billy Buckley the painter had showed up in town to paint the old bank they were turning into a post office. He hung around afterward, painting all kinds of things, and ended up living at the county barn where he was kind of a night watchman and got a room free, a partitioned-off place next to the office. A big restroom, really. The county men came and went, using the toilet.

Billy was hoping to move, but he had a gambling habit that kept him choosing all the time between cards and food. Finding money for rent was just as unlikely as buying a TV, which he dreamed of nightly.

When he arrived at Rooney's, she was sitting in the porch swing giving a ride to a hen that had come out of the bushes after Uncle Pete's purge.

"I'm the painter," he said. "name of Billy Buckley." He wasn't bad-looking except he let himself go, hair and everything, let his clothes get dirty.

"I know who you are," Rooney said.

"I know you, too. I was painting the firehouse the day they vaccinated the dogs."

"They ran mine over. Sweet Sugar Brown. The Schwann man did it."

"I seen it," said Billy. "I seen you run out there and kick his tires. I asked one of those fire guys, Who is that? 'That's Rooney,' he said. 'Rooney Polk.'"

Rooney gazed off in the direction of the Gulf station. "Tires blow up."

"Up?" said Billy. "I thought they blew out."

Rooney laughed. "That's car tires, dummy."

"Oh," Billy said. "Well, I got a pickup." He pointed it out, an old blue truck with the door hanging open. "I brung you some paint samples." He set a little packet down in the swing. "Trouble is, all of em's green."

"You don't like green?"

"I can take it or leave it." He wiped his nose on his sleeve.

"Use your handkerchief," Rooney said.

"I don't normally carry one."

She stopped the swing. "You don't carry a handkerchief? My mother told me, Always have something to blow your nose on."

"Mine told me, Don't blow out the candle till it's time for bed."

"What'd she mean?"

"I was hoping you'd tell me."

Rooney studied his grin. "You want to sit down?"

"Can you move that chicken?"

"Shoo!" Rooney said and tossed the hen in the air.

"Is she gonna go on off?"

"Look for yourself." Rooney made room for him. "Green," she said, "is nature's color. I read all about it in a science book."

"I don't read much."

"I read all the time."

"I watch TV. Except I don't have one."

"I got two," Rooney said.

"You got two TVs?" Billy sat up straight. "What do you want to read for?"

"'Cause I do it good." Rooney leaned over and read his cap. "Blue Star Ointment." Then the writing on his shirt. "Grand Gateway to New Orleens."

Billy tapped his chest. "This right here is the Huey Long Bridge."

"You ever crossed it?"

"Crossed it all the time. Painted it twice. Painted most of New Orlins and half a Louisiana before I left out of there." He watched Rooney rub her teeth. "Say, what are you doing?"

"Doing what I want to. I could paint if I wanted to, but I got a job already."

"At the tailor shop."

"How did you know?"

"I seen you through the windows when I was painting the frames."

"I'm the presser that's been there the longest of anybody."

"How long is that?"

"Ever since school. I press pants and shirts. And tablecloths. Well, I used to press tablecloths till people stopped using em."

"Two TVs," Billy said. "Do you ever watch talk shows?"

Rooney halted the swing. "I'm talking about tablecloths."

"I thought you was through." He broke off suddenly and leaped to his feet. "Git outta here, chicken!"

Rooney laughed. "Git outta here, Joyce, this man is scared of you." She went after Billy. "I guess you're scared of snakes, too. I'm gonna git me one. A bore constrictor."

Billy turned around. "Are you cooking stew?"

"Cooking chili," said Rooney. "As soon as you leave I'm gonna eat me some."

"Why don't you eat it now and give me a bowlful?"

"Why should I?"

"'Cause it's the best-smelling stuff I ever smelled."

"You'll like it better when you taste it. Come in the house. I'll show you my chair. But you have to take a bath before you can sit in it."

A little after nine Pete's telephone rang. He came running back like a mad dog had bit him.

"Git up, Opaline!" She was soaking her feet. "There's a terrible commotion over at Rooney's."

"Has her geese come back? I told you they would. I told you to take em across the river or they'd be back home before you turned around."

"It's worse than geese. It's Billy Buckley!"

"Billy Buckley's over there?"

"You told me to send him."

"Not in the dark!"

"He went in the daylight. They swang in the swing till the sun went down. Then they went in the house and now they're in there, yelling and screaming."

"Call the police!"

"Not twice in one week. We've got to squash it ourselves."

"I'm not going over there with Rooney riled up."

"You're going if I'm going. Put on your shoes!"

They took awhile getting there. Grandma Polk had lathered all over with shaving cream. They had to stop and rinse her off and give her a sleeping pill and then wait around to see if it worked.

Rooney's house was dark when they stepped on the porch.

"I bet she's pregnant already," Opaline said.

Pete banged on the door. "Open up in there!"

Rooney's voice boomed back. "If you're one of those hitchhikers I got a ball bat waiting for you."

"I'm your Uncle Pete Polk with your Aunt Opaline!"

A light came on. Rooney came down the hall in boxer shorts and a long draggy sweater. "What are y'all doing, waking up people?"

Opaline said, "Do you sleep in that?"

"Do you sleep in those pink sausages pinned to your head?"

"All right, girls! Now you straighten up, Rooney, and tell me the truth. Is that painter in there?"

"No, he ain't. He's gone on home where y'all oughta be, tending to Grandma. I bet she's out in the street. Catching a cold."

"You pay attention to your uncle," Opaline said. "We were woken up by neighbors to come and quell a disturbance between you and that Buckley man."

"Yelling and screaming," Pete said.

"Oh, that," said Rooney. "We was watching TV and a chicken flew on him."

"You don't have a chicken."

"I got one old hen that's smarter than the sheriff. I left a crack in the door and she waltzed right in. Buckley don't like feathers and she lit on his head." Rooney laughed. "You should have seen him run! In and out of these rooms. I had to tear off his collar before I could stop him."

"A chicken?" said Pete. "That's all there was to it?"

"Yup." Rooney yawned. "Until he started up again when I asked him later on would he like to get married."

Opaline shrieked. "You hear that, Pete? An absolute stranger and she's ready to marry him!"

"I didn't say marry me. I'd marry a pig before Billy Buckley. He don't read. He don't even know what a handkerchief is."

"Then what did you ask him for?"

"I asked him, Pete, would he like to get married, meaning to any somebody, because if that was in the picture I wasn't going to ask him to move in with me."

"Unlatch this screen and let me sit down."

Rooney led them to the kitchen where the chili was eaten and the bowls still stood, and the crumbled-up crackers.

"You've got to understand one thing," Pete said to Rooney. "There has never been a Polk woman that lived with a man that wasn't her husband."

"The heck there hasn't! What about Aunt Lena? Four men all the time, and quick as one left she got her another one."

"Aunt Lena kept roomers!"

"So am I keeping roomers! I got Buckley cooled off and tomorrow he's coming over here and paint Mama's room foam green and move himself in."

"No, he is not!" Opaline said. "We are selling this house and you are moving to the bungalow by the Gulf."

"I'm staying right here. You said I needed protection and now I got it."

"You won't have it long," Pete told her. "Buckley's got debts all over town."

"He won't owe me nothing. I'm giving him Mama's TV for painting her room and the first month free for doing up mine in sagebrush green. Then he's gonna paint me a big sign to put up by the highway says ROOMS FOR RENT. All of em green. Leaf green, apple green." Rooney grinned at her relatives. "When I make enough money, I'm gonna buy me a gas station."

Opaline said, "You can't do anything without our permission."

Rooney gave her the zebra stare. "I got it, don't I?"

Bear the Dead Away

IRENE SOAKED the handkerchief she brought to Hawley's funeral. She wept out loud. You could hear her all over.

"Stop it," said Katherine behind her glove.

Irene couldn't stop. She kept looking at Hawley piled up in his casket, at the profile of the man she once thought she would marry. His forehead and nose, the rise of his stomach.

"We should have sat further back," Katherine fretted. She wore her gray dress. Irene wore black and open-toed shoes that later picked up sand at the cemetery. She had to lean against a post oak and shake it out, which caused people to stop and start conversations.

"The last thing I needed," Irene said to Katherine. "Trivial chatter when I'm all broken up."

"Understandably so," Katherine said, not understanding. Hawley, after all, was married to Charlotte for no telling how long, and after Charlotte died he didn't take up with Irene again. Added to that, Irene didn't care. She hadn't cared for Hawley since 1940. She said so herself. I'm over him, Katherine. Out on the porch, shelling black-eyed peas.

After the burial service the sisters got in their car, a '56 Chrysler they had bought brand new nine years before. The buggy, they called it. Come get in the buggy.

"What I'd like right now," Katherine said, "is to get out of this girdle. And a nice bowl of ice cream. Let's stop at the store."

Irene sat at the steering wheel. "I made a fool of myself, carrying on like that."

"Nobody minded. Well, I minded a little. Those cousins of Charlotte's kept turning around. Lonie Edwards. She about broke her neck."

"I never saw anyone look so dead."

"Hawley, you mean." A car back of them tooted. "The Walkers, Irene. They can't go till we do."

Irene always drove. If Katherine drove she ran into things. Trying to put the car in the garage, she had to stop in the street to get her bearings, and then drive around the block and get her bearings again. Mrs. Perry on the corner always called Mr. Perry. "Come look at her, Henry."

The Calvert girls, Irene sixty-eight and Katherine seventy, still lived in the house they both were born in, a two-story clapboard on Abingdon Street. The Flashlight Sisters is what they were called for the way they came out on summer nights and watered their flowers. "Like moths," said Nina Simpson across the alley. "Those floaty white nightgowns they flutter around in." They talked in the yard as if they were alone on the planet. *Bring that hose over here!* And Irene's hoarse answer, *I'm soaking the zinnias, the poor thirsty things.*

Katherine taught at the high school for forty-two years. She had students at first who were older than she was. Irene meant to follow her until two burly boys locked Katherine in the toilet.

"It was nothing," said Katherine. "It was only a joke."

"The joke's on you for still hanging around there."

Irene stayed at home and helped her mother. They had one brother, Thomas. His wife's first cousin was Charlotte Edwards, who later was married to Hawley Rains.

Hawley Rains courted Katherine when he first came to town. He saw her walking home from school with her hat on her head and her book satchel swinging. He started coming over in the evenings to sit on the settee and hear her read Browning, which is what Katherine cried over, that kind of stuff. As for Hawley Rains, he had no idea what a line of it meant. He was actually a cowman, stranded by fate in a department store, without money or family and not well-known.

The year was 1916. The war hadn't started, for the U.S. at least, but most people said any minute it would.

Upstairs in the bedroom the sisters shared there was a hole in the floor. Irene—up there dancing—looked down on Hawley and made up her mind to steal Katherine's beau.

"Catch him and you can have him," Katherine said.

Irene waited awhile, to figure out how. She didn't put herself forward when Hawley was around because she was deaf in one ear (from a rising that had ruptured) and because Katherine was regarded as the family beauty.

Irene looked more stern, like Grandmother Moss, whose portrait in the dining room showed a mole hanging off the end of her nose. "Like a booger," Irene said before she was seven. "If it was growing on me, I'd cut it off with a scissors. Or stab myself."

Irene had ideas beyond her age and a deep curiosity that made her read letters not addressed to her and gaze into houses where the shades were left up.

One moonless night after Hawley went home, she was sitting in the dark looking out her window when a light came on in the Gladstones' boardinghouse across the street. A man entered the room and sat down on the bed and read from the Bible (the Song of Solomon, she later decided). He read rather poorly, in her opinion. At least it took him so long, she caught herself dozing. At last he stood up. He went to the mirror and, garment by garment, denuded himself.

"Katherine," Irene said, "come here and look."

"I'm asleep," Katherine said.

"It's a naked man."

In less than five minutes Katherine Calvert had fallen in love.

The nude man they observed flexing his biceps was a train engineer, accustomed to disrobing in moving cabooses. He had just come to town. He was H. K. Adams, called Hank by Hawley because he knew him from before when the two of them were boys living off in West Texas, minding cattle for a rude-crude man they both were kin to. It was Hawley himself who introduced Katherine.

Hank stepped into the picture just right for Irene. As soon as she saw how the land was going to lie, she sent a note to Hawley at his place across town. A shack, to tell the truth, that he was needing to get out of before the roof fell in.

Dear Mr. Rains. Those were formal days. *Could you spare me an hour by the West Fork bridge where Parker's old smokehouse stands on the bluff?* Where the violets grow was what she wanted to say, but it didn't seem fitting, coming from the pen of the sister of Katherine whom he hoped to espouse. *At four this afternoon?*

She sent the note by Tom and told him to wait.

"Wait for what?" Tom was her nephew, her brother's boy.

"For an answer, of course. And maybe a tip. He may give you a nickel."

"If he don't, will you pay me?"

"I'll pay you now."

That's how it happened he chased all over and finally found Hawley under the feed store helping Chester McManus set traps for rats.

"Can you meet my aunt by the West Fork bridge?" Tom had lost the note, but remembered the gist of it.

Hawley scuttled right out, thinking the boy meant Katherine. "What time shall I be there?"

"You're late already, but I'll tell her to wait."

Hawley flipped him a dime and rushed to his domicile to put on a jacket.

Hawley Rains, it was said, had a bitter upbringing. First he lost his mother, as many boys did in that day and time. Women gave birth and languished, and aunts were brought in. Hawley's aunt was a pain, a great-aunt at that.

"He won't last the year," she told Hawley's father.

Hawley claimed to have heard her, though still in his crib. "She was as close to a buzzard as a woman can get."

Other bad things befell him, he told Irene. His house burned down. He had to drop out of school. He lost two toes when a copperhead bit him. "That's the reason I limp."

"It's not a bad limp." In Irene's view it was no limp at all.

"Then my father got married to Lena Mae Fancy. A strumpet," said Hawley, looking depressed.

"A trumpet?" Irene said, her bad ear toward him.

"A lady of the evening," Hawley said harshly. "A woman of the street." He would never have mentioned such a subject to Katherine, but it was Irene's way to probe into things, and she had gotten Hawley started and he couldn't stop.

She was a very young woman, but she seemed much older from having wormed out of people their most private secrets. She was affected, too, by the peculiar excitement of being with Hawley alone in the woods. (The violets weren't blooming.

They were still underground with only their leaves showing, tender green hearts poking out of the weeds.)

When Hawley arrived at the meeting place, it took quite awhile to set things straight. He expected Katherine and he found Irene who had given Tom a quarter for chasing through town to deliver a note Hawley paid a dime for but never received.

"Well, what do you want?" Hawley said in a snit.

"A talk," Irene said, "when you've finished your supper." She brought forth a basket, a four o'clock tea, but now it was six.

"There's ham here," she said. She was horribly nervous. "And a nice creamy cheese." She had made it herself from day-old curds strained through a cloth into a pan on the drainboard.

"It's too cold for a picnic," Hawley said.

"We can eat in the smokehouse."

"The smokehouse!" He laughed.

It turned out they had to. A shower came up and battered the grass down. They had to run. Irene, small and fleet, and Hawley behind her, gasping for breath. He hadn't kept fit. He smoked cigarettes he rolled himself and sat up all night reading out-of-town newspapers he unwrapped off the china at the store where he worked.

He spoke of the store while he gobbled up sandwiches. "I hate the damned place."

"It's a stepping-stone, Hawley."

"It's a prison," he said.

She had calmed down a lot. "What would you do if you didn't do that?"

"Raise cattle. Ride horses. I'd own lots of land."

The smokehouse, they found, was not a bad place. No windows to speak of, but a wide bench to sit on and a table before it.

"For slaughtering pigs," Hawley surmised.

Eating ham after that was a trial for Irene. She nibbled on bread she broke off with her fingers.

"A ranch is your dream?" She twined a dark curl. "I dream of a lover."

Ham stuck in his throat. The woman was loose! An unvirtuous girl who somehow or other was Katherine's sister. "Water," he croaked.

She offered him Ovaltine.

"There's a skin on the top!"

"Skim it off," she said and finished her thought. "But you can't have a lover if you've never been kissed."

All she knew on the subject she had found out in books. "Trysts on the moor," she explained to him throatily.

They could talk about anything after that. And did, at length. His childhood, his chicken pox, her scarlet fever. They had to open the door and let the moon come in, and then sit close together with Hawley's arm protecting her shoulder.

"You don't like apple pie?"

"I like lemon better."

One thing and another and finally this: "There's something, Hawley, I came here to tell you."

"I know what it is." He was all buoyed up by the curls on her neck and the smell of her skin which he took to be lotion but really was youth. "You want me to kiss you."

"Yes, I do." She could see the way now, how it all would work out. "But in fairness to Katherine, I must tell you this first." She breathed on him gently with a celery breath. "H. K. and Katherine have fallen in love."

His processes stopped. "H. K. and Katherine?" Blinking and swallowing—everything stopped. "Hank? Not *Hank.*"

"Hawley?" she said. This was somehow amiss, this clubbed look he was giving her when moments before her mere preference for pies had held him enthralled. "It's best, don't you think, that you hear it from me?"

He took down his arm and sat like a chunk of marble granite. "You're lying," he said.

"*Lying?* I'm not! The minute you leave, he crosses the street and sits where you sat. On the settee," she said. "And he *kisses* her, Hawley, which you never have!"

"You don't know that I haven't."

"Sisters talk." She saw at once the error in that. "Except me, I don't. I'm mum as a tomb."

"Oh yes! I'll bet."

She came back at him haughtily. "Hawley, the Snarler. Is that why she dropped you?"

"You're a minx and a troublemaker."

"You're a big bag of wind!"

She went around then, tossing scraps from their supper out the door for the foxes. And sighing big sighs as if her spleen hurt her.

In awhile Hawley said, "It's bad enough to lose Katherine, but Hank Adams, you know, was the best friend I had."

He wasn't, she knew. They had never been friends. They punched cows together and that was all. Cheered, she said, "Think of it this way, as just a short chapter in the book of your life."

"It's the end," Hawley said. "I'm ruined in this town. I'll have to go West."

"Go? You'd leave? Don't you have any pride?"

"It's been trampled upon, ground in the dust."

"Nobody knows that except you and me."

"And Katherine and Hank."

"Well, of course they know, but they don't know that you know. So what you must do"—she was small and exquisite, he suddenly noticed—"and do it at once, is to go and tell Katherine that you're terribly sorry, but you've fallen in love with somebody else."

"Who?" he asked.

"Who!" she exclaimed. "If you can't answer that, go jump off the bridge."

He reached for her arms. "Come sit on my lap."

"You big damned fool!"

"Young ladies don't curse."

"They do on occasion." She was weeping fat tears, as much for his touch as the way he had humbled her. "Let go at once or I'll call the constable."

"You'll have to call loudly, he's miles away." Hawley gathered her close. He had never held Katherine, she knew for a fact. Never kissed her forehead or pressed her lips. "You're a brave little thing."

She wept all the more.

"Have you loved me for long?"

"You big-headed jackass. I should slap your face."

"Better than that, touch me gently." In barely a whisper, "As I'm touching you."

Hawley Rains. He paid proper court for the rest of the year, a gallant romancer in the guise of a cowman. They would have been married, but the war began.

H. K. went first and then Hawley went. He came back at once because of his foot that was missing two toes from the copperhead bite.

"They won't take me," he said, still blank with astonishment. "But I'm joining up anyway. The ambulance corps."

Irene couldn't believe it. "But you don't have to go!"

"I do, Irene. My country is calling."

"It's not calling *you!*" There were men staying home. Her brother Thomas for one.

"He has children, Irene."

Edward Scranton, the blacksmith, he wasn't going. Or Hiller, May's husband. Or Bertie MacMahon.

"Bertie MacMahon is seventy-nine."

While H. K. and Hawley were fighting the war, Irene and Katherine plotted the wedding. One wedding for both of them was how it would be.

"In the parlor, Katherine?"

"Of course in the parlor. We'll deck it with sunflowers."

"Shall we ask Maidy Howard to play the piano?"

Their mother would oblige by making the cake. The girls themselves planned to sew the dresses.

For sentiment's sake Irene wanted Tom to carry the rings. "He carried my first message to Hawley, you know."

"Do I know!" Katherine said. "You met in that smoke-house and a whole string of dogs followed you home."

"I came home alone and went up the back stairs."

"You were Hawley's new love. I knew that for sure when I got into bed and a ninety-pound sausage was snoring beside me."

It was all going well, the wedding plans and the war, which was just about over. Then in half a week's time Mr. Calvert died and then their mother died too, in the flu epidemic. Young Tom died as well, and his father, Thomas, and two of their neighbors on Abingdon Street.

Soon after that, word came back that H. K. was killed in the Milestone Battle. The word came through the railroad, secondhand to Katherine because Katherine, of course, was not part of the family and not a fiancé because H. K. when he left had not yet bought a ring.

Irene tried to explain when Hawley came home. "We can't marry yet. It's too soon after everything."

He strode around in the new way he had that the war had given him. "It's too late for some things." Too late to get a start on a herd before winter, to find a place he was sure would have water and grass. "We'll just go to West Texas and rent a place. Maybe by spring—"

"Maybe by spring we can marry," she said. "But I can't leave now with the state Katherine's in."

She saw it written all over him how desperate he was for life to get going. He had seen it bleeding out in too many French ditches. "Life gets away!"

"I know it does, Hawley." She had seen for herself its vanishing act. "But we have to think about Katherine. Her parents have died, and her brother and nephew and H. K. too. I have to stay here till she's back on her feet."

"That might take a lifetime."

"Or only a year."

"A year, Irene! Don't you understand, I've been through a war."

"If you don't know, Hawley, what we've been through, then you don't know anything."

That's how they parted, in one bitter evening that ended with Irene going out early in the morning to Hawley's old shack to tell him all right, she would go to West Texas if they took Katherine too.

Hawley, of course, had already left. Cleared out, as they say, with all that he owned that was worth the trip.

She wrote him a letter and waited to mail it till she had an address. The next thing she heard, he had married Charlotte Edwards. It was Hilda who told her, Thomas's widow.

Hawley came back once, when Charlotte died. He brought her to rest in the Edwards plot, where there was room for him, too, if the time ever came. He'd been thinking lately, he told an old friend, that he might never die. Out where he lived, on top of the Cap Rock, the sky had no end and the hills that reared up had no beginning. They came out of the earth from its other side and the wind sawed them off.

He stayed around a few days, doing business, he said. When he married Charlotte, he married land. He had cattle and horses, a ranch house with a pool.

"A pool in the desert?" Katherine said.

"It's not really a desert." Irene had a talk with him in front of a store. She stepped out and stopped him. "Hawley," she said.

"Why, Irene, is it you?"

"Who else would it be?"

He wore a gold watch chain across his stomach. "Do you remember that cheese we ate in the smokehouse?"

"I remember the ham."

"I seem to recall I choked on that ham."

"Not quite," Irene said. "Ovaltine saved you."

He left the next day without coming to see her.

"He may write," Katherine said. She was shelling peas from a brown paper sack spread out in her lap. She was still teaching school, you might say in her prime.

"He might tell you finally why he went off. He lost ground in my book, I can tell you that, running away when you waited for him all through the war."

"I'm over him, Katherine."

"Well, so am I, I'm over H. K., but you just like to know when there's a mystery involved."

"There's no mystery to it. He was ready to go and he packed up and went." Irene dealt with it that way. It took years, but she did it.

"He wanted that land Charlotte had."

That was Katherine's theory. Irene let her think it. It saved her from figuring out what really had happened and taking the blame for Irene's never marrying. Katherine herself, as she liked to say, was married in spirit to the only man she could ever love.

"I was fated, Irene, to find my love early and lose him forever."

In the grocery store Irene bought a quart of chocolate revel and a medium-sized bag of pale little cookies.

"Go take off your girdle," she said to Katherine back at the house. "I'll dish up the ice cream."

"Don't do it too soon. I want to change my shoes."

Katherine climbed the stairs in the way she had now of stopping twice before she got to the landing.

Irene stood at the sink and looked at the yard full of wilting daisies. "The yard needs water," she said out loud. She talked to herself whenever she could. She believed most people did but wouldn't admit it.

"The flowers at the graveside will be wilting too." Those beautiful glads buckling over, and the asters—"Well, asters never last."

She caught sight of herself in the windowpane. Swollen eyes, her mouth pulled down. "Fool," she said, "you've cried your eyes out and over what?"

Over Hawley, of course. "The love of my life, lying there dead."

That big bag of wind was the love of your life?

She saw Hawley again mounded up in his coffin, gold chain across his stomach, his lodge fob on it. She crossed the kitchen and set out the bowls and the silver spoons Grandmother Moss had left for their trousseaus.

In actual fact she had never met the man meant only for her. If he came along, she didn't see him—because Hawley Rains had flashed across her life like Halley's Comet and left the sky dark for fifty-one years.

"Now *that*," she said, "is something to cry about."

She stopped still and thought. *I did cry about it.*

It wasn't Hawley she had mourned at the church! It was her own stalled life: her ship run aground while still in the harbor, her passion unspent, delights unexplored that she had nosed out of books and gleaned listening at doors. Sweets glimpsed in letters, but never tasted!

She let out a howl. Hawley got his dream, his ranchland and cattle. He went out and claimed it. "But you," she groaned, "you settled for hope!"

Wretched hope had kept her in port, had siphoned her youth away and left her to wither.

Then just as quickly she saw another truth. "But I've *outlasted* hope!"

With Hawley dead, nothing was going to happen that she had spent her days waiting for, after Charlotte died, and in the years before when she contemplated quarrels and a heated divorce, foresaw a stabbing even, saw Charlotte running away from the Cap Rock, drowning, marrying a count and moving to Europe.

"That's all over now." She let out a cry. "I can lay down hope for asters to wilt on!"

Katherine called from the stairs. "What's wrong down there? What's all the racket?"

"Nothing. I'm singing!"

"*Sing*ing?"

"Hymns!" She mopped up her tears, thinking once again what a sensible person she'd always been, like a round-bottomed toy no one could knock over. The foxiest of foxes. A violet underground, green leaves trembling.

She heard Katherine coming. "I bet you've let the ice cream melt on the table."

She swished her black skirts. "Oh no, my dear sister. I'm setting it out now."

The Oil of Gladness

"LISTEN," Champ said. This was last Thursday evening over the phone in front of a grocery, a Seven-Eleven over on Wayside, close to the park. I go there for milk and sometimes for bread or for beer now and then. I do my big shopping at H.E.B. when the specials are on. I was raised that way, to be saving with money.

"Listen," he said. "I have to be gone till the first of the week." I was calling him up to find out what he wanted for supper that night. I had thought about burgers, but if he'd rather have Mexican then I needed tortillas. I planned to ask, too, what time he was coming. He was off that day, always on Thursdays. He works on his own, putting sheetrock in houses. Sometimes he's off for a week or two if jobs are scarce. Once for six weeks he did nothing at all. No money came in. He was like a zoo animal, pacing around.

"Where are you going?" I thought I could ask, I'm wearing his ring. Well, I've tried it on. It's still at the store, but I feel it's mine. It was promised to me.

Champ took offense when I asked that question. For the first time since I've known him (nearly two years) he decided to keep private something between us. He practically growled. "I've got things to tend to."

"Oh, excuse me," I said. I was wishing like mad I hadn't called. Would he have called me? Would I have gone on and cooked and then sat there and waited? "It's just if you're going to go off, I want to know where. If I don't have that right, then forget it, Champ." A man going by in an orange-colored sweater gave me a look.

"Minnie," Champ said. My name is not Minnie. It's Anne-Marie. He got started calling me that because I called him Mickey once, for the way his hair grows up high on his forehead in Mickey Mouse curves. I was kidding with Mickey, but Minnie stuck. It ought to sound tender but most times it doesn't. It sounds like a put-down. On Thursday it sounded like MOUSE in big letters, saying, Mind your own business.

"I'm going to Lubbock. As soon as I'm back, I'll call you," he said.

"When will that be?"

"Minnie." Big sigh. "On Sunday. Or Monday."

"Well, have a nice trip." I hung up the phone. That's spiteful, I guess, but I'm not prepared to be shut out like that and have him get harsh. I've had enough of stern men. One minute they're jokey and then they're cold. I want my guy to be steady, the same all the time. That's why I liked Champ the first time I met him. And then he did this.

Back home I was blue. I had chores to do: clean towels to fold and ironing to sprinkle (I iron on the side for a lady downstairs), but with Champ dropping out—that's how I saw it, like he'd gone up in a plane and got sucked out an exit—I felt at loose ends. That's a tired way to say it, trite, they would call it in my literature class, but it fills the bill (another trite phrase. *Cliché* is the name for it, I've recently learned). But you know how it is when you've planned your evening and then you don't have it, how rotten you feel.

I don't think I ate. Or maybe I did. I know I went to bed early and couldn't sleep. At half past eleven I got up and read. Since I'm taking this course I have lessons to do. I have my job, too. I clean apartments for money. I use my own gear, my personal vacuum and electric broom and all my attachments. I have a rack in my car Champ built to hold everything. It comes out on wheels I can pull along. It holds my supplies, my feather duster, my rags and solutions.

I needed sleep bad, but I read for an hour, a couple of essays, one about toys that was kind of sweet, and another on Hebrews. "The Oil of Gladness." That's a quote from this letter Paul wrote to the Hebrews. Paul, the Apostle of Jesus, you know.

"God, who at sundry times and in divers manners spake in times past unto the fathers by the prophets."

It's heavy stuff. But it gets better as it goes along, the idea being that in olden times when God wanted to say something he spoke through these prophets that everyone looked to to get the message. But now he has his Son, Jesus the Christ, the heir of all things, who speaks for God.

He speaks in our hearts, the essay says. And God, who adores him, anointed Jesus with the oil of gladness and set him above the angels. "For to what angel," Paul wants to know, "did God ever say, *'Thou art my son, today I have begotten thee'*? Did ever say to an angel, *'Sit at my right hand till I make thy enemies a stool for thy feet'*?"

There's a whole lot more, but what it boils down to is that Jesus endures. When everything else goes, *thou remainest*. Reading those words was a comfort to me when Champ dropped out and didn't say why, just went off to Lubbock.

After the essays, I wrote to Jeanie. Jeanie is my daughter who I don't ever see because she's afflicted. (My grandmother says that's an old, old word that means broken in spirit, which is not Jeanie's trouble, but I let it go.) I like to write Jeanie letters, though she can't read anything and can't understand them. I just have a strong need to write to my child.

I do it for me, but I think somewhere down the line something will come across to her. She'll be holding one of my letters and the sun will be shining on it and she will know in that instant that she has a mother and I care about her. In some remote way she will know this. Maybe at the same instant I'll know she knows—and it will carry us through till somehow we get together.

The odds are, of course, that we never will. She is seriously impaired. They told me when she was born she will never learn anything, never be a person out on her own. She is not put together in a normal way. She is not one of those beautiful retarded children that you can dress up and give a good hair-cut and hardly anyone will notice there's anything the matter.

Jeanie isn't like that. But where her mind is concerned I keep on hoping. Champ says it's not silly, it's my right to think that, and how does anyone know that it might not come true? One thing that helps: whoever gets the letters never sends them back.

I was sort of like Jeanie myself at one time; a person locked up in a dull-looking child. My parents were kids and they just went off. I stayed for a while with various folks until my grandmother found me. She had several husbands—not all at one time. They came and they went. But they were all hard men. She had a failing that way, of marrying men that made our lives miserable.

I guess I got Jeanie to have someone to love. That's what they say now in psychology courses about young girls having babies and no way to care for them.

The state took Jeanie. She's a ward of the state.

As soon as I could, I went out on my own. I've done pretty good, but what extra I have goes to my grandmother, in a nursing home now. There's nothing left over for Jeanie but letters. At least not yet, until something happens.

One thing that happened, the very next day after I phoned Champ. I dropped my keys. It was the craziest thing. I was mailing Jeanie's letter in the drive-by slot outside the post office. I had the keys in my hand to my Friday apartments—the ones I clean—and instead of the letter, I mailed the keys.

I sat there in the rain and heard them clank down the slot. Cars lined up behind me started in honking. I had to go around the block, park and get out and go in for help. The help was nice, unlocking the box with the rain coming down, but they let me know what a pest I was, which was no news to me. I've been a pest all my life to someone or other. Champ is the latest, it looks like at least, him going off to Lubbock, sneaking, I'd say, and not telling me why.

I guess I was crying (I couldn't tell which was, the windshield or me). The fact of the matter, the night before when I went to bed I vowed in my prayers I was going to endure, like Jesus, you know, and when I went to work I'd spread the oil of gladness over every piece of furniture I dusted that day and not think once of Minnie the Mouse or Champ the Louse. And there I was, whining, "Champ, oh Champ," as if he could help me, way off up there.

Ashamed of myself, I bucked up a little and caught a green light, but at the first stop on my schedule (I work only for bachelors who get up and leave and get out of my way) the man was still there.

They're supposed to be out. That's in the contract. And there he was sleeping when I unlocked the door. That isn't all. He had a girl with him.

Do you know what I did? I backed straight out and sat on the buzzer.

Tat-a-tat-rat till the rat poked his head out.

"Oh hell, is it Friday?" A young blond guy. A big disappointment. I thought he'd be older. He sounded older when he called last spring. See, I never do see them, the guys I work for. It's done on the phone. I don't advertise. Clients tell clients. Word gets around if you do good work.

On the phone he told me his name was Tom Gruen (like the old Gruen watch my grandmother had), and we made our arrangement: Friday mornings at eight he'd leave my check on the bar and I'd leave the contract. Which I did—and he did, and has done ever since. He has never been there, stretched out in the bed with a girl beside him.

Tom Gruen, in fact, was my favorite client. He puts away his stuff. No shorts in the shower or jock straps on the sofa. Some men I work for could never have girls stay overnight.

Another thing, too. I like dusting at Tom's, examining what's around, looking it over. It's not like at my place where

I have an assortment: nine china cats, a cypress-knee cowboy (Yosemite Bill) and a stuffed armadillo I bought a child's Stetson for. I have a doll, too, a beautiful bride doll that sits in a high chair pulled up to the counter. I have a shelf full of bears and four Dancing Raisins. I like fun around me.

Tom Gruen's place has a holy air. What I mean is, it's quiet, his stuff is all quiet: tall simple lamps (no anchors or mermaids holding them up). Just a single bowl by itself on a table. He has books, all kinds. He has *icons,* he calls them. (I left a note one time and asked what they were.) They are framed in a row, holy pictures, maybe some of the prophets. He has nice rugs too. You get to know rugs in my kind of business.

You could say we're friends, Tom Gruen and me. So last Friday morning what I did was pardon him.

"This one time," I told him, "I'll come back later."

He took it in stride. "Thanks a mil." And he shut the door.

I went over to Shadowway, the next place I go. I was a few hours early, but who was to care? The other Fridays (the Friday bachelors) were all off at work like they should have been. As long as I cleaned, they wouldn't care when. It felt funny though, all out of order, eating my lunch in Bailey's apartment and watching my soap at Gentleman Jim's. (I call him that because at Christmas one time he left me a diamond, a fake one, of course, just as a joke, but sometimes I wear it. It's big as an egg.)

The things these guys leave around tell you a lot. It's like working a jigsaw (puzzle, I mean). You can put them together from what they leave in their wastebaskets and drop on the floor. At least that's what I thought until I finally met one.

I did all my places and then I went back at a quarter to three to Tom Gruen's place.

Do you know, he was there! Tom Gruen was there, still hanging around.

I was mad as hell. "It's against the rules. You're supposed to be OUT!"

He looked kind of sick. Hung over, I guess. "I'll go if you like, but I'd rather stay here."

"I don't clean apartments that have men in them."

"I can understand that." But he didn't budge. He had on a sweater I hadn't seen in his closet, and shoes with no socks. Short little shoes. "You aren't Tom Gruen!"

He looked surprised. "I'm Rafer," he said.

"Rafer?"

"Ralph." He turned kind of red. "Tom is my brother. You didn't know that?"

"I don't even know Tom. *He's* never here. Mr. Rafer or Ralph, you'll have to get out."

He finally left. "You'll be through in two hours?"

"Two and a half. It's my day to clean cabinets."

"You can skip that," he said.

"It's my day to do it."

He came back, of course, before I was finished. That girl being there had messed up a few things, and Ralpher had too— or Rafer, whatever. He wasn't his brother, I'll tell you that.

He sat down with a beer while I cleaned up the kitchen. He was looking for work, and lonely, I saw. He didn't like cities. He'd come from the country (I had figured that out) and he was going back, too, as quick as he could.

"Where's Tom?" I asked.

"Tom's gone to Lubbock."

I sank in a chair, as they do in novels, in Tom Gruen's kitchen where I'd never sat down. "What's going on here?"

"What do you mean?"

"Does his hair grow in curves, like Mickey Mouse's?"

"Whose hair is that?"

"Your brother's, of course. Is he ever called Champ?"

"Hey—" Rafer stared. "Are you on something, lady?"

"The point, don't you see, is I know someone else that's gone off to Lubbock."

"People do that, don't they? It's a fair-sized place."

"But *two* people I know? And both of them there at the exact same time?" I gave up on Ralph. "You don't get it, do you? Oh, skip it," I said.

I'd dreamed a fantastic outcome in just a few seconds: I'd made Champ and Tom Gruen one and the same. I'd had us get married and move into Tom's place (a little surprise he'd been saving, he said) and then I found out that Tom knew a doctor who could reconstruct Jeanie.

I think of such things when I'm running the vacuum. When I'm mailing a letter and drop in my keys.

I looked at Tom's brother, alert at the table for what I'd say next. "Are you Rafer in town and Ralph in the country?"

He blinked a few times. "Sort of," he said, an overgrown kid, maybe not even twenty, with no business at all bringing a girl to his brother's apartment.

"You ought to decide which one you are. I heard a preacher one time preach on names. At the end of the Bible, in the Revelation, the Spirit addresses the overcomers. He says, I'll give you a white stone with a new name on it and no man will know it except him that gets it." I gave Ralph a hard look. "Names are important."

He slunk off to the living room and put his feet on the sofa.

I finished my work. When I picked up my check I went in and got him. "Come home with me. I'll fix you some supper."

Rafer took to my place like a duck takes to water. (Another cliché I've got to weed out.) He got down on the floor with Yosemite Bill. He took the Stetson hat off the armadillo and looked for the hole the bullet had made.

I said, "No such thing. He died on the highway. I spent forty-five dollars getting him stuffed."

We had a good meal: cheese enchiladas and Wolf Brand chili. I found out about Tom. An archaeologist.

"When he moved to this town he didn't even know there was such a thing. He was selling shoes in a mall," Rafer said. "Then he started to college."

A little thrilly chill skittered over my backbone. "I'm going to college. I've learned about writing. Essays and letters, to Hebrews," I said.

"College will change you," Rafer predicted.

"It won't change me. I like things like they are. I'm engaged to be married."

I had a little picture of Jeanie to show him. Not really of Jeanie, of some other child I found on a bus, but I didn't somehow. I put it back in my billfold and made us some coffee.

He left after that, and I went to bed.

I said my prayers. I said, *Jesus endures* and *Thank you, God, for getting me through one whole day without Champ at my elbow.* I was going off to sleep when the telephone rang.

Guess who it was, calling from Lubbock.

He was back to himself, all ready to tell me how he happened to go there. He had got a big job of apartment houses, with more in the offing if this one worked out. He hadn't wanted to say so for fear he would jinx it.

"The only trouble," he said, "I'll be gone for a while."

"How long is a while?"

"Six months. Maybe more."

"Shall I mail your clothes?"

"Minnie," he said, "you're still mad at me, aren't you?"

"No, I'm not mad. I'm glad for you, Champ." The truth of the matter, I felt greased all over with the oil of gladness.

I didn't know why until I hung up and got back in bed.

With Champ not around I'd have time to study. I could take more courses, archaeology maybe. On some sunny Saturday I'd go and see Jeanie and let us hold each other instead of a letter.

One other thing I've thought about since. If Champ comes back and says Minnie to me, I'll say to him: *Anne-Marie.*

Housekeeping

MISS ELOISE BANNISTER owned a house on Florida Street she wanted to stop renting. She wanted to sell it. Or burn it down and collect the insurance, or let it go for taxes. She did not want to scrub the walls again and rake the muck out of the kitchen and lay down new linoleum and fix the faucets.

So when the man called up she said, "You could probably get a room over in Payne. Seven miles away. A larger town."

The man wasn't interested. "Sounds to me like sleeping on nails."

"Like what? A nice place like Payne?" Then she got his meaning. He was thinking *Pain!* A homonym! Forty years of teaching language in the Grover Public Schools and she'd never noticed. Chagrined, she said, "It's spelled with a *y*."

"Oh, I see." He seemed pleased about it. "I had a relative once, Payne with a *y*."

He cleared a gravelly throat. "The thing is, I don't want a room. I want a house with a yard. I like to mow grass."

He was crazy. Or young. "There's a yard," she said patiently, "but it isn't all grass." Most of it was weeds. The back part was bushes that formed a little thicket where redbirds nested. Owls took shelter there. On cloudy days it got black as night inside that thicket. "It's hard work, you know, to keep a yard looking nice."

Hers didn't, not the Florida Street yard or her own that backed up to the thicket and ran on down to Tennessee. The yards hadn't looked nice since Mr. Cooper got lame and she had to hire a boy who didn't know beans.

"I don't mind hard work," the man replied. "And I have plenty time."

You *are* young, she thought, and probably a drifter. She closed the conversation. "I don't want to rent, but thank you for calling."

He answered politely, "Thank you, ma'am," and hung up the phone.

After supper Eloise told Grace when Grace came across the street to help pick figs. "It was unfriendly of me. New people moving in. I know they need houses."

"But you need to sell."

"I don't *need* to, Grace." Grace was trying again to find out about her finances, if she had any money beyond her teacher retirement. "I'm just tired of taking care of it, getting broken things fixed and dealing with deadbeats."

"He might not be a deadbeat. You could hardly tell over the telephone."

"He sounded very nice."

"He looked nice, too."

"What do you mean?"

"I saw him at Maggie's." Grace's niece across town. "I drove over there to see if she had any eggs and to find out about Sissy, if she'd had her baby or not. When I got out of my car he was getting into his truck. Abel Brown, Maggie said. String bean type. Cap on his head."

"Well if this isn't funny! What did Maggie say?"

"Said no more eggs till the weather cools off."

"I mean about Mr. Brown."

"Don't you care about the baby?"

"Grace—yes. Here, give me that bucket. We'll go up on the porch and have a talk."

"This is my bucket, Eloise. I brought it from home. And what about these figs? If you leave 'em till morning, you won't have a one a bird hasn't pecked."

"All right then. We'll talk while we pick."

They didn't though. What settled the matter was a wasp that stung Grace on the end of her elbow and sent her home.

She called back in a little while to say she hadn't died of anaphylactic shock.

Eloise was in bed with the radio on. "I'm glad to hear it."

"You can laugh if you want to, but it happens all the time. People's throats swell up and they can't catch their breath."

"If you were worried, Grace, you should have said so."

"I wasn't worried. I've been stung by wasps ten thousand times. What I'm calling to tell you is to lock up your house. Maggie told that Brown man where you live. Straight through the block from the Florida house. On Tennessee. A woman alone."

"Did she tell him that too?"

"I don't know if she did, but it's in the phone book. Eloise Bannister. Does that sound alone?"

It did, thought Eloise. Alone and lonely. Once you started to think about it, you might not stop. "I don't think I have to worry. You said he looked nice."

"You can't tell a thing by how somebody looks. And something else, Eloise. Sissy had a baby girl last Wednesday morning at four o'clock and nobody called."

"Would you have wanted them to at four o'clock?"

"They could have waited till seven. Instead they waited two days and I still had to go and find out myself. After all the presents I've given that girl."

"I'm sorry, Grace. I expect they forgot in their excitement."

"Well, don't you forget about locking up."

"I lock my doors every night at nine."

"I lock mine at eight. Earlier than that if there's a strange man in town, nosing around."

"You never did tell me why Mr. Brown was at Maggie's."

"He wasn't *at* Maggie's, Eloise. He was out on the sidewalk. That's all there was to it."

"Did he stop just to chat?"

"He stopped," said Grace, "to ask about the rent house next door to Maggie."

"The Blackman house? He wouldn't want that."

"That's what Maggie told him. Then she told him about your place."

"You can tell her next time that my place is for sale."

"Tell her yourself. She'd love to hear from her favorite teacher."

"Her favorite teacher was Isabel Martin."

"Well, I can't argue about it now. My program is on."

"Do you think I'm keeping you? You called me!"

Eloise got up at daybreak to finish picking the figs. She went out in her nightgown to the side of the garage and stood in the wet grass without any shoes on. She intended to pick the front of the tree first and be around back when the paperboy passed, but before that could happen a pickup truck turned into the driveway.

A man got out. String bean type. Cap on his head. "Good morning ma'am."

Eloise stared, something she had taught children never to do.

"Excuse the hour." He crossed the grass. "But I saw you were out."

Out in her nightgown! But at least it wasn't one of those see-throughs. "I came out early to beat the birds."

He nodded approvingly. "Birds do love figs." He was a man about seventy. Or seventy-five and well preserved. On the telephone he had sounded forty.

How had she sounded?

She stood up straight, like a woman, she hoped, who had on underwear. "Mr. Brown," she said. She was pleased to see him jump. "As I mentioned on the phone, I'm not renting my house. I plan to sell it."

"With a hole in the roof?"

Eloise jumped.

He said more gently, "You didn't hear the wind? Blowing hard in the night?"

She hadn't heard anything. She had gone to sleep thinking how paranoid Grace was and hadn't waked up until the clock in the living room was striking six.

"A good-sized limb struck your porch."

"A limb," she said. Why not lightning? "I'd better go and see." She set off grimly in the direction of the thicket.

Brown came after her. "We'll go in my truck." Without laying a finger on her he herded her toward it and got her in.

She came to herself when he slammed the door. "Wait!" she said. "I have to go in the house and get my wrapper."

"And hunt for your slippers. And stop by the mirror and comb your hair." He backed the truck. "Just sit tight. This won't take a minute."

"On the phone," she said, "you had a few manners."

"You can take a quick look, and I'll bring you right back."

She sat speechless beside him until they rounded the corner and she saw her house, a child's drawing of a house: the front-door-mouth, two windows for eyes. "I don't see a limb."

"You can't see from here." He drove around the back. "Look up yonder." The limb lay on the roof like a torn-off leg.

"I don't see a hole."

"It's the size of a skateboard. I climbed up and looked."

"You climbed my roof?"

"On a ladder, of course. I carry a ladder." He pointed a thumb toward the bed of the truck, to saws and hammers and everything else.

"Are you a carpenter?"

"I can do carpenter work. And painting and such. I can fix this rip for next to nothing. There's plenty shingles in your garage."

"You went in my garage?"

"And also the storeroom. Looking for decking." He shot her a grin. "Found some, too."

"Mr. Brown," she said, "you haven't been hired." She was nearly naked and foolishly seated in this man's truck, but she said it anyway, and said something else. "What are you up to?"

He looked straight at her. "Up to filling my time."

She had stared down enough schoolboys to think she could believe him. "You've been riding around this morning, searching for damages?"

"On the chance. Yes, ma'am."

"Stop calling me ma'am! I'm not a hundred."

"Didn't think you were." His blue eyes twinkled. "Thought you might be seventy."

"That's wrong too." But it was close enough to give her a shiver. "If I hire you for this job, when can you start?"

"In the next five minutes."

"How much will you charge?"

"A fair and honest price. You can count on that."

"Make it fifty dollars and you can do it."

"Make it sixty-five, depending on the decking. And extra, of course, if I have to buy nails."

Eloise walked home. She insisted on that in case Grace, as usual, was looking out a window. She told Abel Brown she walked around barefoot to strengthen her arches, but on the path through the thicket the lie about killed her. She had to sit down twice, once on the bench where she read her devotionals, and one more time on the stump of an ash tree where fire ants bit her on both sets of toes and up one ankle.

When she got to her house, she took a cold bath mixed with baking soda and didn't eat breakfast until a quarter of nine.

"I'm all off schedule," she told Grace when Grace called up to see why she was at home and not at the library. She went every Friday, over to Payne, to check in books and check out more.

"I'm leaving right now." She drove around the block. Mr. Brown wasn't visible, but his truck was there. She said out loud. "Sixty-five bucks. Mr. Abel Brown must think money is water."

In Payne she discovered the library closed. For roof repairs. "Wind damage," a man said, standing on the sidewalk.

She drove home bitterly and went to the store for fire ant bait, and lemons and sugar and jars for preserves. She had to go back for corn pads and Tums and to stop at the post office and run by the bank. At one o'clock she began on the figs.

The first batch scorched because Grace telephoned to see who was hammering.

"Mr. Brown is at your rent house? What's he doing there?"

Eloise explained, leaving out the nightgown. "I have to go, Grace. I'm cooking preserves."

"Did you peel the figs?"

"I like the peeling left on."

"Tell me this: do you think he's handsome?"

Eloise heard the lawnmower sometime later. She had paraffin melting and couldn't go out. At four-thirty she went, crossing her lawn (beautifully cut) and passing through the thicket where she threw down ant bait. Emerging at the rent house, she found the grass mowed there, the roof mended, and the truck leaving with the broken-off limb.

"Mr. Brown!" she called.

Mr. Brown hopped out. "Miss Bannister," he said, "you're wearing shoes."

"A few hours barefoot is all it takes." She saw Grace was right: he was a nice-looking man, in an elderly way. And a gentleman, too, or else he would have mentioned clothes as well as shoes.

"The roof looks nice," Eloise told him.

"It's going to look better when those new shingles weather."

"You mowed both lawns."

"I like mowing lawns."

"You're hauling off the limb."

"That's part of the roof job."

"Well, that's very nice," Eloise said.

"Well, I'll see you tomorrow."

Her brain spun around. "Tomorrow? What for? I'll pay you now." She opened her purse, a little snap-mouthed affair her mother once carried. A miser's purse, Grace liked to call it. "How much do I owe you?"

"No hurry," he said. "One or two things still need to be done."

"You've done too much. More than I'm paying for."

"Step around here. I'll show you something."

He pointed out the screens. "These screens are torn."

"I've noticed," she said.

"Have you noticed the steps?" He put a foot through one without the least effort. "It's things like this that bring down the price when you sell a place."

"I know, Mr. Brown, but I am not putting money into this house."

"You have to put money in to get money out."

Eloise sighed. This sweet little house was her parents' honeymoon cottage. Hers, too, she once imagined. Had she imagined it since? Maybe one or two times before she was fifty. Or whenever it was her periods stopped.

"Look," Brown said. Another step crumbled.

If she burned the place down she might go to jail. "How much would it cost? The screens and the steps?"

Abel Brown clutched his throat. "I'll be glad to tell you over a drink of water."

Mr. Brown stayed for supper.

He played the violin. Her father's violin that she kept on a shelf in the living room. She sat him down in there because the kitchen was a wreck: jars of fig preserves all over the drainboard, dirty pots in the sink and shiny places on the floor their shoes stuck to.

He didn't play well. Old strings, he said. But he brought out a certain note now and then that put a lump in her throat and she let him go on though it drove her crazy.

She apologized ten times for having him work all day without any water. He told her eleven times he did have water. He had a whole jug full, but he drank it all up. He'd only been dry, he said, for thirty minutes.

Thirty minutes was too long, Eloise said. He had the

biggest feet she had ever seen. Size sixteen was what she guessed. Big hands, too, floating over the violin, tucking it under his chin.

He stopped playing at last and told her quietly, "I'm going to get your supper."

"Why, what do you mean?" She jumped out of her chair where she had been sort of dreaming, going up a ladder into somebody's attic.

"You can't cook in that kitchen."

She didn't tell him she hadn't intended to. She ate cereal for supper with a banana sliced over it. Tonight she had planned to eat a cantaloupe.

"Where will you get it?" she croaked out at him.

"I'll drive over to Payne."

"Seven miles," she marveled.

"They have a deli over there at a convenience store."

He had learned a lot about Payne since yesterday. "It's not a big deli."

He laughed out loud. "Do you want a big supper?"

In her embarrassment she said, "Get enough for yourself."

While he was gone she slammed things around and cleaned up the kitchen. She put a cloth on the table and got out napkins. Feeling like a fool, she went outside and picked a bouquet of blue plumbago, knowing while she did it the blooms would drop off and the prickly stuff underneath would latch onto everything.

Of course Grace was out, picking up twigs. She called across the street, "Did you finish your figs?"

"Yes, they're fine."

"I'll come have a look."

"I'm expecting Mr. Brown in just a few minutes."

"Mr. Brown?" Grace halted.

"I have to pay him for his work."

"Are you giving him flowers?"

"I'm trimming the bush."

"Oh," said Grace. "Well, have a good time."

Eloise did enjoy herself. Up to a point.

Mr. Brown brought shrimp, boiled and peeled, and potato salad. Men, she had been told, love potato salad. She herself seldom bought it, and never in hot weather for fear of ptomaine. Possibly the shrimp were tainted, too, though they tasted all right. If later in the night she had to get up and go to the hospital, she had a clean gown and an insurance policy.

"Miss Eloise," Brown said when he had eaten the cantaloupe she served for dessert. "Driving over to Payne I had a thought about your house."

"Did you?" she said. They had drunk a little wine from an old green bottle she had opened at Christmas and now he was filling their glasses again.

"You know I live in a trailer."

She didn't know, but she said, "How nice."

"It's not any bigger than a sardine can. I haven't been out of it for more than a year."

"You've been traveling?" she said.

"Traveling all over."

"What made you stop here?"

"I came down the highway and saw the lake."

Full of dirty brown water, Eloise thought. If she were able to travel, she would go to the mountains.

"I'm parked in that camp next to the bridge. It's not a bad spot, but I'm sick of that trailer."

Eloise sipped wine. "I can't rent you my house. I'm sorry, Abel." *Abel,* she heard. Heard it leap from her lips like a frog in a fairy tale.

"Eloise." He smiled. "I'm going to help you sell it."

"Are you in real estate too?"

"I have a proposition."

"A proposition!"

"A business deal." He patted her hand, which she picked up quickly and put under the table. "I worked it out on the way to Payne."

She calmed down slowly when she heard what it was.

He had an idea he would live in her house. Instead of paying rent, he would renovate it.

"Insane," she said.

"Room by room. I'll start in the kitchen. I'll tear out the sink and then do the cabinets."

"You'll do no such thing."

"You can't sell a house that's falling down and get anything for it."

"I'll sell it that way or not at all."

"Just listen a minute."

"No," she said.

He got the violin and picked out a few notes. "It's a honeymoon cottage."

She came to attention. "How did you know?"

"They all have that look."

"There are others?" she said.

"Maybe none quite as nice." He put down the violin and tried her preserves from a dish on the stove left out as a sample. "Is there lemon in this?"

"Of course there's lemon."

"But no vanilla?"

"Certainly not."

He sat down again and said like a grandfather, "Eloise. You have a fine house you're letting rot down."

The lump came back. "How can I help it?"

"You didn't listen. I'm offering free my priceless labor."

"And materials?" she said. "Are those free too? If I wanted to do it, I can't spare the money."

"Borrow it, dear."

"I never borrow."

"Your credit's no good?"

"I don't owe a cent and never intend to."

"Oh, too bad." He seemed truly sorry. "You're squeezing your pennies and letting your dollars run out the door."

"I have supported myself for a good many years!"

"And nicely, I'm sure, but you might have done better if you'd sold this big house and moved to the small one."

"You're full of ideas."

"Good ones, too." He plucked again on the strings of the violin. "Do you know that song, 'The Beautiful Old Things'?"

"No, I don't."

"I don't either. I wish I did." He got out of his chair and strolled to the door. "Thank you, Miss El, for an interesting evening. You'll understand if I move along now."

"Wait," she said. "I want to give you your money." She turned to get it. When she turned back around he was already gone.

She didn't sleep all night. Her thoughts ran amok like squirrels in an attic. She got up at four and went out to the kitchen to clear a place in the pantry to put the preserves. Then she mopped the floor and sat in the dark with the violin. At the first sign of day she put on a housecoat and slippers and went to the thicket.

Above her bench a redbird was singing.

"*Cheer up,* yourself!" she told the bird. "You don't have a house that's falling down. Or a head like a pumpkin from Christmas wine." She stared at her feet speckled with ant bites. What should she do? Keep saving her money for Death with Dignity? Keep putting aside for the Lingering Illness, for women coming in to cook and clean and trim her chin whiskers and privately bathe her?

Or should she blow it? Spend it all reviving the cottage. New sinks, new screens, no telling what.

Was it only yesterday she was picking figs when Abel Brown drove up in her yard?

He drove up now. In the rent house yard. She saw through the bushes his descent from the truck, his strides toward the porch. He began prying boards off the steps. Like he owned the place!

She jumped up and burst through the yaupon. "What are you doing?"

"This has to be fixed." He seemed unsurprised that she had appeared. "I'm doing it now and getting it done with."

She saw a diagrammed sentence up in the air, *with* dangling off like an extra foot. "It's the Sabbath," she said.

"Can't a fellow pull nails out of boards on the Sabbath?"

"People are sleeping!"

"I bet in Payne they're not." He laughed at his pun. "All right. Come on. Let's go and drink coffee till the sleepers get up."

*   *   *

"This is twice you've pulled this," Eloise complained. He was toasting bread without even asking.

"You don't really mind, do you, Miss El?" He buttered the toast and spread on figs. "What's going to happen to all those jars of this wonderful stuff?"

"I give them for Christmas."

"That's a long way off. Christmas," he said.

"You may take one now if that's what you're wanting."

"That's it, all right. Cold winter mornings figs'll sure taste good."

Eloise sat and wondered: where will he be when winter comes on? In Florida maybe. *Or in the Florida Street house?* She saw it happening like a train bearing down on Eloise Bannister tied to the tracks.

"I told you a lie," she said without meaning to.

"About your money?" He looked over his cup. "You have some, do you?"

"Of course I do. A woman alone. Who would look after me?"

"The government," he said and poured more coffee. "Or some good man."

"I'm past all that."

"You are if you think so." He sat back and grinned. "If you found the right man you could be Porch-Bannister."

She answered him, bristling. "Funnier still, I could be Brown-Bannister."

"Miss El!" he said. "Do you want to discuss it?"

"Certainly not!"

"That's worse than *ma'am,* saying *certainly not* all the time." He went to the pantry. "Did you say two jars?"

He came out with three. "I lied to you, too." He set the jars on the tabletop. "I didn't plan the renovation on the way to buy supper. I planned it all day, even down to the colors. Confederate blue in both the bedrooms. White on the woodwork." He went a step further. "Crazy quilts on the beds."

She turned from the sink where she was washing the dishes. "This is going too far."

"Yup, it is. It's way out of hand." He crossed to her side. "Are the church people up? Or should I go on to Payne and come back later?"

She dried her hands. "I'll pay you what I owe you and there won't be any need to come back at all."

A stillness came over him. "If that's how you want it, it's sixty dollars."

"Did you have to buy decking?"

"Nails have gone up."

She took her snap-mouthed purse out of a cabinet. "I'm paying you seventy."

"Suit yourself, but I might say this. I wouldn't keep money like that in the house."

"I'm not afraid."

"You never can tell who might walk in the door."

A string bean man. A cap on his head. "You did a good job fixing the roof."

"My pleasure," he said. He saluted her sadly. "Ever need a good kiss, give me a call."

She went around all day calling him names. Impertinent jackass. Impudent fool. She avoided Grace by not going to church. In the late afternoon she slipped off to Payne and went to the movies. And then ate shrimp and potato salad.

He would come back, of course. To get his preserves.

By Tuesday he hadn't. Wednesday either.

She got in her car and drove to the bridge. Across the water she could see the trailers lined up in the camp. Which was his? Where was his truck?

She came home and telephoned.

The attendant told her he pulled out Monday.

"What's the matter with you?" Grace asked in the kitchen, her eyes wide open, like a questioning cow's.

"Nothing is the matter."

"You weren't at church. You haven't swept the sidewalk and now you're mending. You never pick up a needle unless you're sick."

"Sewing makes me sick."

"So why are you doing it?"

They went into the living room and sat on the couch,

Eloise discommoded by the violin not in its place, and Grace agog at this turn of events.

"Mr. Brown," said Eloise, "has gone on his way."

"Mr. Brown?" Grace said. "Well, I can't say I'm sorry. He couldn't be trusted."

"You don't even know him."

"I've seen him, Eloise."

"On the sidewalk at Maggie's."

"In and out of your house."

"You spied on us, Grace?"

"Of course. Wouldn't you?"

Eloise brought cake and warmed-over coffee. She made a clean breast of things. Half clean anyway, omitting the night-gown and the kissing remark.

"So the problem," said Grace, "is he tore up your steps and left without fixing them?"

"More or less." Eloise raised her chin. "The truth is—I miss him."

Grace leaned closer. "In what way do you mean?"

"Someone coming and going. It livened things up."

"Of course it did. You by yourself."

"You're by yourself."

"I have family, Eloise. You haven't anyone."

"It's true, Grace. I have suffered a loss."

"Oh, my dear …"

"But it's nothing to pity. What I've had is a lapse. Natural,

I think, for a woman my age who has never been married, who has never cared to be involved in any way with a man." She hesitated. "But now, late in life—"

Grace said quickly, "How old are you? Seventy?"

"Now late in life a kind of panic sets in."

"A panic?" said Grace.

"Panic and worse. A dormant silliness."

"A what?"

"A silliness, that has waked up all at once and wants to dance."

"Dance!" exclaimed Grace.

"Wants to kick up its heels! Haven't you ever felt that?"

"I guess I have. Once after Roger died there was a butcher at Four Star who had lovely lips."

"Lips?" said Eloise, thrown off the track.

"I used to dream of those lips, coming down on me. His name was Fritz."

"I remember a Fred."

"That might have been it."

"What happened, Grace?"

"It passed without consequence."

Eloise said quietly, "This might pass."

"It will. Give it time. You can't know a man in only two days."

"Five," said Eloise.

"He's been gone three of those."

"Will you have more cake?"

"It's delicious," said Grace. "Did you bake it for him?"

"It's been in the freezer since the last bake sale."

"In that case," said Grace, "I think I baked it." She turned back to Eloise. "I know what would help. If you were to see Mr. Brown as I see him."

"Oh, I don't think so."

Grace persisted. Her view of the matter was that Abel Brown was a competent con man whose only aim was to get the cottage.

"Get it?" said Eloise. "What do you mean?"

"Own it," said Grace. "Fix it up and sell it and scoot out of town."

Eloise felt better, hearing this nonsense. "He couldn't sell it. I have the deed."

"He could marry you, couldn't he?"

"If I were drugged and shackled!"

"You're sounding more and more like a woman in love."

"It isn't love! It's not even affection. If it's anything, it's loneliness, Grace."

"I'm lonely too. But I wouldn't dive off the high board just to cure it."

"No cures have been offered."

"You're lucky there. Look how he worked things. Smooth as a tick's back, mowing your lawn, buying your supper."

"Schemes, do you think? Right at the start I asked what he was up to."

"What did he say?"

"He likes to fill his time."

Grace snickered. "Any fool can lie. He looks like a man who would stop at nothing."

"How can you tell?"

"By the way he walks."

"Oh yes, I see. One foot, then the other."

"Use your common sense, Eloise."

"Do you think I have any?"

"You have more than me."

Eloise was astonished. "Am I hearing things?"

"Of the two of us, you're the practical one. I rely on you."

"After today, you'll think twice about that."

"I'm glad you told me. It makes you seem human."

"I didn't before?"

"Not as much as most people. You always have answers to everything."

"Grace, that's ridiculous."

"It's not your fault. Teaching does it. Haven't you noticed? Teachers get bossy."

"It's getting late, Grace. It's time for supper."

"Are you asking me to eat or telling me to leave?" Grace got up. "Whichever, I'm going. It's Bingo night."

She paused beside Eloise. "Do you think after this I could call you Ellie?"

"Not this week. Probably never."

"There," said Grace. "That's what I mean."

* * *

On Thursday Eloise went around in her wrapper, reading old letters and playing the piano. She put a Vicks plaster on her chest and then peeled it off.

On Friday she dressed and went to the library.

Abel Brown was there. She didn't know it. She wandered around, reading blurbs on the mysteries until somebody said, "Here's Mr. Brown's water. Who's going to take it?"

"Mr. Brown who?" It popped out like a frog.

"Up on the roof."

"I'll take it," she said. "I'm going that way."

He had barely come down before she was after him.

"It's too high up there for a man of your age!"

"Why, Miss El," he said, "you've put on your shoes and stepped out of your bailiwick."

"Because I read," she told him severely.

"I read, too. That's how I found out there was work over here."

"Have you moved your trailer here?"

"To the Family Campground, where I'm slightly out of place, but nevertheless." He shook sweat from his brow. "Is this water for me?"

She steered him to a tree. "Are you trying to kill yourself? It's ninety degrees."

"It's a hundred and twenty up on the roof."

"Then quit and go home!"

"I'd rather die up there than cooped-up somewhere in a nursing home."

"You aren't ready to die."

"The trouble is, when you do get ready, they rarely let you." Eloise pressed on. "You forgot your preserves."

He lifted gray eyebrows. "Is it safe to come get it?"

"Come about four. You can fix the steps."

Eloise fixed a picnic and took it out when the hammering stopped. She meant for them to eat on the cottage lawn, but they ate in the thicket because an early thrush mixed-up on the seasons was singing its heart out and she wanted to hear.

They sat on her bench and spread out the food on a folding table.

"This is good," Abel said about baked beans and wieners.

"Try some of this." Mustard chow-chow she had made herself.

With the meal under way, she made an announcement. "I have halfway decided you can live in my house."

"Halfway?" he said.

"I have to know first if you're a con man."

He whooped at that. "Do you think if I was I'd tell you yes?"

"Are you or aren't you? Tell me straight."

"I am not a con man."

"You understand, don't you, what I mean by that?"

"I think I do. A liar and a cheat who might slicker you out of whatever you own."

"That's it exactly." She folded her hands. "And you say you aren't? Can I believe you?"

"It's the truth, Eloise. Would you pass the grapes."

She ate the banana she had previously intended to slice over cereal and eat in the kitchen. "Grace says it all fits together for you to be crooked."

"Grace." He frowned. "Grace from across the street? Who ducks into the garage when she thinks I've seen her?"

"She thinks your walk gives you away, that you were smooth as a tick's back, the way you worked me."

He nodded agreeably. "I did some of that."

"Mowing the lawns? Bringing me supper?"

"And playing the violin. I thought you'd enjoy it."

"You didn't play well."

"I played well enough to put you to sleep." He ate a cracker. "I worked you another time, to get the preserves."

"Grace thinks you want to get my house."

"I want to live in it awhile and see how it feels to get out of that trailer."

"What if you like it?"

"Maybe I'll buy it."

"Do you have any money?"

"Enough," he said.

The bird sang again from a farther place, whistling purer than air or water.

Eloise said: "What have you been doing for most of your life?"

"Smoking for one thing. But I gave it up." He leaned back and thought. "I drilled oil wells. I built a few houses. Mostly," he said, "I've gone around looking." He gave her a grin. "For more lawns to mow. What about you?"

"I've been right here. Teaching," she said. "And picking figs."

"Why didn't you marry?"

"Why should I marry? I was in love with teaching. And I had my parents."

She picked a leaf and folded it neatly. "Have you given any thought to the shape of the year?"

"The year?" He chuckled. "I can't say I have."

"Have you never noticed that it's winter on one end and on the other end too?"

He took her hand, a child's hand in the palm of his, and squeezed it lightly. "If you were in charge, how would you arrange it?"

"I'd start with summer and end with spring." She let his thumb trace the moons of her fingernails, though her mouth was dry and her heart was knocking. "Grace says—"

He gave a mild groan.

"She says I ought to know you longer before I trust you."

"You can tell Grace people our age can't waste time on long engagements."

"Engagements!" she said.

"Just a manner of speaking, Eloise."

"We are not engaged."

"We are not," he agreed.

She let her heart calm down before she spoke again. "Have you ever been married?"

"Once," he said. "For about thirty minutes."

"Why didn't it last?"

"We didn't like each other."

"Abel," she said, "you may live in my cottage if you tell me truthfully you have no interest in making a match."

"A match." He smiled. "You mean like a couple? Miss El," he said. "I will never legally or criminally seize your house."

"It's not the house alone." She went ahead fearfully. "It's what you might think because I'm letting you live in it."

"I might think you care for me."

"Yes," she said. "I wouldn't want to mislead you."

He chuckled again. "You *don't* care for me."

"I don't care for marriage."

"Would you care to explain?"

"I'm not sure I can."

"Try, why don't you?"

She started slowly and gathered steam. "I've lived by myself for too many years. I have to have my own room. I like to read late. I get up and take medicine. And I'm used to playing the radio all night if I want."

He waited quietly.

"And sex," she burst out with a bravery unknown to her. "The very idea of it gives me a stomachache."

"Scares you," he said.

"Scares me to death."

They listened to the bird in the thicket again. When it flew, Abel said, "I've lived by myself most of my life. I need my own room. I watch TV until two in the morning. I get up and take walks. And sex at my age is not to be counted on."

"Well," said Eloise, "I'm glad that's settled."

"It's good," he agreed, "to have it out of the way."

They sat awhile longer. When the fireflies came out she began putting things in the picnic hamper.

"Would you like more tea?"

"Tea? No, thank you." He stopped her hands from folding the tablecloth. "Tell me again about your year."

"I'd start it in June."

"So that would mean that right about now it's the middle of January?"

"Yes." She laughed. "Can't you tell it's cooler?"

"By July, your time, I'll be through with the house. Is that long enough to get over a scare?"

"Six months? Oh, no. No, I don't think so."

"How long will it take?"

He felt her tremble. "Maybe till Christmas."

"Dear girl," he soothed, "July *is* Christmas."

"I mean next year."

"Miss El," he whispered. He put an arm around her. "I would never rush you but by any calendar it's time we kissed."

"Oh, Abel, we can't! It's not dark yet."

"Close your eyes, sweetheart, and you'll see that it is."

In the Little Hunky River

IN THE SUMMER of 1968 when she turned fifteen, she made up her mind to get the canoe out of the storehouse and put it in the river, the way her parents had done when she was twelve. When they tipped over in it and fell out and drowned.

The only thing was, she couldn't do it alone. She needed strong arms to get the canoe off the wall and into the water. She needed a boyfriend, but she had no prospects. "What's the matter with me?" she asked BoPeep.

"Less see," Peep said. Peep was nearly eighty, but she did not wear glasses. She did not drag her feet the way old people did, and she still ran the house and cooked the meals.

"You bossy, that's one thing."

"Not around boys."

"You bossy just breathing."

She was Anna Catherine on her birth certificate, but after her parents died she began calling herself Page. "Page Gage," she said to Aunt Florrie. "Only one letter is different. And also, it rhymes."

Aunt Florrie said, "It rhymes, dear, but it isn't musical."

"It doesn't have to be musical," Oliver said.

Uncle Oliver, her guardian, was refreshed by the idea of choosing a new name. For himself he thought of Madison, or possibly Pierce. Pierce Gage would have no trouble shaping up a lumberyard about to go under.

"What else?" said Page. "Besides being bossy?"

Peep considered. "You taller, that's two things, and you makes all A's."

"Grades count?" Page flounced off, but she came back later when Peep was washing grit off the mustard greens. "I really need a boyfriend. Can't you help me?"

"What I gonna do? Go call one up?" Peep dried her black arms and sat down in the rocker that was put in the kitchen for her to take naps in.

Page sat on a footstool her grandmother had made: seven quart-sized cans upholstered in padded chintz and sewn in a circle. "If I had a boyfriend I could take down the canoe and put it in the river."

The Little Hunky. A minor branch that flowed below the bluff the house sat on. She and the boy would float along until something (what?) upset the boat and they both fell out. Not to drown. Simply to discover how her parents had drowned when her father, T. G., knew how to swim and should have saved himself as well as Janet, her mother, but somehow didn't and left Anna Catherine to grow up an orphan in Oliver's house.

"But I can't ask a boy I don't even know who doesn't know me. Can I?" asked Page. "Do you think I could?"

"Uh-huh," said Peep, already dozing.

The day of the drowning Anna Catherine had watched T. G. and Janet with the canoe over their heads, crossing the lawn, disappearing. Oliver, watching, too, gave her a quarter and she walked to town and drank a soda. When she came walking back, Peep took her in the kitchen and she found out then that her parents were dead. It was like a story in a book. It was like the carnival moving on and leaving their Ferris wheel in Whitman's pasture. As if they didn't need it. As if they could have a carnival without it.

"So you think," said Page, "that I could just go out and sit in the swing and the first boy to come along, any old boy..." On any afternoon? Maybe even today? Except it was Saturday and Oliver was at home. On a regular day no one would notice her hailing a boy from the front porch. Peep lay on her bed in the afternoon, and Florrie stayed upstairs and wrote in her room.

Florrie, Oliver's wife, was a celebrated poet in Garrison County and known all over for unsolicited recitations at social gatherings. Poems, of course, and lines from stories she started writing but never finished. *Angelique rose before the day was ready to be looked at, while it was yet slouching along in its black overcoat, its hat pulled down over the stars.* On other occasions she quoted scripture. Once at a bridal shower: "To whom will you flee for help? And where will you leave your glory?"

She did it, Oliver said, when conversations got boring.

"She do it," Peep said, "to get the floor."

Peep spoke without restraint about the Gage family.

Oliver's father, Anderson Gage, gave BoPeep her name when he was four years old. When he died, he left her the house her family had always lived in and a sum of money to use as she pleased.

"Your grampa put it in his will," Peep told Page. "And put in why. A person name a person, he like savin their life. After that, he gotta take care of em long as they live."

The summer that Anna Catherine became Page she spent most of her days with Peep in the kitchen. "Was it very much money my grandfather left you?"

"Be more now than when it was give me, in spite of all the kinfolks I'm doling it out to."

Page ate a brown fig. "Do any of your folks live in Garrison County?" (She hoped to be around when the doling was done.)

Peep, however, had run them all off.

"Always hounding me for nickels and dimes. I told em though, if they got their tails in a crack they could drop me a postcard, and if it wasn't their fault I'd send em a money order."

"What do they do if it is their fault?"

"If that ever happens, I'll let you know."

Peep told Page that Miz Florrie wrote poems because she couldn't write checks. "She a tenant farmer's daughter and they didn't learn her how."

"That's not the truth, is it?"

"She was ten years old before she had any shoes. And going on twelve before she rode in a car."

"But you like her, don't you?"

"I likes Miz Florrie. Likes her up in her room doin her writing. Likes her a-plenty when she goin out the door."

Peep told Page that when Oliver was young he lost a new Ford car trying to go up Pike's Peak in the middle of winter. "Don't nobody do that but jackrabbits and crows." In the spring he went back to dig it out, but there wasn't a sign of it, up or down.

She said Oliver coming home on a dark night from a bachelor party ran over an alligator and thought for three days he had killed a man. He might have carried that burden to his grave except for a newspaper reporter who came along later and took a picture. GIANT GATOR FLATTENED ON FRIDAY.

"Why didn't Uncle Oliver go to the police?"

"The po-lice!" laughed Peep. "Who what's drunk is gonna do that?"

"Uncle Oliver was drunk? Does he get drunk often?"

"Far as I know, he ain't drank since."

Page ate another fig. "My father drank. Did you like my father the way you like Oliver?"

"Don't like nobody the way I like Oliver. He my baby."

"He's not really your baby."

"I got him borned. I slapped the breath in him when he come out blue. Now he watch over me like his papa did. Ever morning fore day he come and knock on my door. 'You in there, Peep?' And I says back, 'Where else would I be?' But if I don't answer I know I can count on him. He gonna put my teeth in and straighten me up fore he call anybody to tell em I'm dead."

BoPeep in her chair opened her eyes. "Turn on the fire under the greens."

Page said, "I can't right now. I'm thinking about something."

"Think about greens. Put em on low and wake me up in time to make the cornbread."

Anna Catherine wore a child's dress to her parents' funeral, one her mother had made, too short and too tight for a twelve-year-old, but Page wanted it on her, wanted to wrap herself in it and cover her head if she possibly could.

At the cemetery she held Oliver's hand and stood next to the statue of Grandfather Gage. When he was seventy-one he commissioned his own monument, a large granite chair with a figure of himself sitting in it. Big stone fingers, stone fingernails. Two marble eyes stared down at Anna Catherine, who knew how to swim, but when her parents were drowning she was down in the town ordering a soda, choosing a straw from the tall glass canister the straws leaned out of when she lifted the lid. She was stopping at the feed store to weigh herself, and swinging the hanging fern pots at the Garrison Hotel.

She wept so loudly Oliver took her to the car and sat with her there until the service was over.

At the house afterward friends ate sandwiches and speculated.

"Janet stood up suddenly before the canoe went over."

"Bob Gordon saw her from his house across the river."

"A bee might have stung her."

"Or stung T. G. and she stood up to swat it."

"It was Fate pure and simple."

"It was predestination."

Anna Catherine sat on the stairs. As soon as she was older she would go down in the river and see what was there. Seaweed, she thought. And water snakes, tangling her parents' arms, wrapping around them. It might be necessary to take a knife.

When everyone had gone, Florrie stood in the dining room, in tears again. "Oliver, do you see? Do you see what has happened to our great and wonderful family?" Years before when she married into it, seventeen members lived on the same street. "They have all gone from us. They have lain down in darkness and left us alone on this withering plain."

Peep spoke from the kitchen. "You still got cousins living in Atlanta."

"They are not Gage cousins! All of the Gages have departed from this earth except we four. We are the remnant."

"Don't count me. I ain't a Gage."

Florrie lifted her voice. "You are a Gage in spirit! You've been in this family longer than any of us."

"The cat by the fire don't eat at the table."

"You are welcome, BoPeep, to eat at our table at any time. As you already know. And if you don't, you should be ashamed."

"Miz Florrie," Peep said and went back to the dishes stacked on her drainboard.

Florrie crossed the room and kissed Anna Catherine. She recited a long passage about the waters of Babylon and the hanging of hearts on willow trees, and then she went upstairs to change into her writing clothes: an assemblage of scarves she wore over pajamas.

Oliver said, "She won't come down again until tomorrow."

"So us," said Peep, "got to git ourselves together. Anybody want coffee?"

Anna Catherine said yes, she'd have a cup.

Oliver brooded over scattered plates and crumpled napkins. "I'm going back to the cemetery and see if the graves are covered over and the flowers put on. Anna Catherine, honey, do you want to go?"

"She havin her coffee!" Peep said.

So he rode off alone down the boulevard and into the trees.

It was a bad idea, his father always said, to plant trees in a cemetery, especially oaks, with their roots going everywhere, burying themselves and crowding out people.

It was a lumberman's view Oliver didn't share, like so many things about the lumber business, but it was too late now to walk away. He was the whole cheese now. He was Gage & Sons all by himself.

He fixed his attention on his Oldsmobile. Princess Pat, he called it, for no other reason except pure love for its faithful service. When he bought the Olds his mother was still alive, and his dear sisters too. Also Aunt Jessie Fields under those cedars and others he rolled by who had passed away while his odometer was turning.

At the two fresh mounds he halted the car and sat looking at the graves blanketed with flowers: white narcissus blooms and other yard blossoms friends had brought over in the morning wrapped in green tissue paper and laid on the porch, an old custom he hoped never died.

People died. His father, his mother. Amelia and Mary. Now T. G. and Janet. Gone, as Florrie said, from this withering plain, leaving him to be last, the last Gage male, with no hope in hell of producing another one.

He meditated on that sorry fact until he found himself wondering what Peep would serve for supper. More funeral food? Or grits and eggs?

The sun going down lit his father's monument. Without thinking about it, he crossed the lot and climbed up and sat in his father's lap.

The stone came from Italy. His father had gone there and chosen it himself. He was there six weeks, posing for the sculptor.

A prosperous man, Oliver thought. "And I," he said aloud, "can't afford a hammer."

He laid his head against his father's chest and began speaking about the state of their business. Of Gage & Sons. "Down now to Son. *Run*-down. Inventory down. Work force down."

He gazed at leaning tombstones pocked with lichen, and artificial poinsettias six months old.

"T.G.," he said. "T.G. was taking money."

He half-expected the stone chair to crack. He wished it would, wished it would throw him down the hill and into the river where he could lie, unaccountable, on its slimy bottom until he was scooped up and put in his grave.

"The first I knew was last Wednesday morning. T.G. broke down over a big stack of bills, and I saw the whole picture, saw it all at once: the gambling and the drinking. He wasn't spending Janet's money like I thought he was. The Yard money was buying those cars and fancying up his house.

Gage & Sons was tumbling down. And what was I doing? I was walking around, joking with customers, and not even noticing how few there were."

A mockingbird sang, running through a repertoire of ten or twelve birds and a barking dog. A setter, thought Oliver. Old man Jessup's. It never shut up.

"T. G. promised to pay it all back. He'd get a loan from Janet's father against her inheritance. Of course, first, Janet had to agree. I don't know if she did. That was Friday. They drowned on Saturday."

Foolish, the evening buzzed. *Foolish, foolish,* as he himself had been numbers of times in his silly life, imagining himself wise, picturing himself as somebody to envy.

Oliver closed his eyes, letting exhaustion take him down the hill, into the water where what had happened had happened. Whatever it was.

When he woke again, night had come on. A man Peep had sent was tugging on his foot, calling out fearfully, "You awright?"

Page said at the table after cornbread and greens, "What is everybody doing this afternoon?"

Peep announced that after cleaning up the dishes she was going to her house (a smaller one back of the big one) and have a lay-down until half past three. Or if she felt like it, half past four.

Florrie said dreamily she'd be going upstairs to work on her piece, a rhyming saga about the Gage family and the Karankawa Indians (a cannibal tribe which, according to her research, had eaten a Gage).

Oliver's intention was to put up a ladder and start painting the house.

"What a ridiculous idea," Florrie said.

"You too old," Peep said. "You come crashin down, we'll have to shovel you up."

"Forty-six is old? Men my age are running three-legged races."

"Exactly," said Florrie. "Do something entertaining on your afternoon off."

Page laughed. "He'll need another leg. Are there volunteers?"

"Seriously, sweetheart," Florrie said. "You had a man from the Yard come and do the scraping."

"At great expense. And now he's through."

Florrie heard his regret. "The way to handle that is to have him come back."

"Florrie dear, that's the way I would have handled it if we still had money."

He saw her startled look. "Have we run out of money?"

He had pledged to Florrie when he took her from the cotton fields that she would never have to worry about anything again. As far as he knew she never had. He told his troubles to Peep and told Florrie nothing. Protecting her, he called it when Peep disapproved. But now all at once—since noon, when he propped that damned ladder against the house—a rebellion had started, a powerful urge to unburden himself, to open the cage and let the tigers run out.

Page should know her father was a thief. Florrie ought to be told how her bungling husband was running the family business with a blindfold on...

"Are we?" Florrie repeated. "Out of money?"

"Not entirely. We're not in the poorhouse. We. Uh. We just have to be careful because business is bad."

"We have to Cut Corners," Page put in.

Florrie looked around the table. "Haven't we been doing that for years and years?"

"*We* has," said Peep, and went out to the kitchen.

Florrie had not applied herself to Cutting Corners because in her view she spent no money. She did not buy groceries; Peep did that. She did not drive the car so she bought no gas; and she rarely bought clothes, preferring to costume herself in the elegant antiquities she found in the attic.

`She turned again to Oliver. "Shouldn't we by now be making a recovery?"

"Recoveries take time."

"Oliver," she said, "what happened to the money?"

His head swam as if he were already tilted against the second story. "It's too complicated to get into now."

"But Uncle Oliver," said Page, "what did happen to it? Didn't my father have money?"

"And your father, Oliver. All of the Gages have always had money."

Peep boomed from the kitchen, "Money come and it go!"

"Like a tide," said Oliver, barely audible. The tide right now was pretty far out, but there were indications things might get better.

For the last three years he had hung on by his toenails, shuffling small payments among his creditors and trading on the Gage name until he had worn it so thin he felt naked behind it. Then a piece of luck: a buyer came along for T. G.'s house and paid straight-out cash. A few weeks later Oliver gained another inch by selling Janet's car and her custom-made furniture for way more than he figured they were worth. Risking those profits (plowed back into the business in Anna Catherine's name) he had bid on the construction of a clothing store and a small addition to the elementary school. To his surprise, both contracts went to Gage & Sons, inspiring one of his old carpenters to come back to work. Luck bred luck—or so it seemed. Or so he *hoped,* with the ladder waiting for him.

He pushed back from the table and said with false heartiness, "Time to paint."

"Oliver," said Florrie. "You hate heights."

"I used to hate heights. I'm over it now."

She rose beside him and kissed his cheek. " 'May the Lord your God hold your right hand.' "

"Thank you, Florrie."

"And I," she said, "will hold the ladder."

"Florrie, no. You go on upstairs and work on your Indians."

"I think I will enjoy painting the house."

Peep gave a little moan. "You hear that, Lord? If she gonna help, I gotta help too. She gonna want ice water ever five minutes."

Page said, "I wish I could help," thinking of the Little Hunky, of going down in it where the water snakes were. But it was the right thing to do, a high-minded thing Grandfather Gage was bound to approve of. And she had prayed for a helper this afternoon. He might be on the way. "I'll be out on the porch. Reading a book. For school," she said.

"School done out," Peep reminded.

"It's a summer project, which I mentioned to you, but you must have been asleep. Uncle Oliver," Page called, "be careful on the ladder."

Oliver was careful, but he fell to the ground about a quarter to three.

He fell at the same instant that Fate (or possibly predestination) brought a white black man into Garrison on a bus.

He was the boy Page had prayed for, although he was older, a man of twenty-one in a suit and tie. But he looked like a boy. He was nervous as a boy. He asked for directions and started on foot toward the boulevard.

Page was not reading her book when he arrived. She was pedaling her bicycle back from the hospital. When she saw a stranger standing on the porch, she was too full of everything to connect his appearance with the prayers she had prayed. It was the coat, she thought later, and the suitcase he carried.

She threw down her bike and rushed up to him. "If you're looking for the people that live in this house, they're all at the hospital. I've been there, too, but I've come home to call the Yard to send a car after them. And also," she panted, "to see if Peep left the burner burning under the coffeepot."

The young man said, "Miss BoPeep Bailey? Is she in the hospital?"

"She's at, not in. But this is not her house. Her house is around back."

"Where it should be, of course," the young man said, but he said it politely. He had a golden tan as if under his skin candles were burning.

Page looked at his suitcase. "Are you selling insurance?"

He said he was not. "Is Miss Bailey ill?"

"Are you from the North?"

From Chicago, he said.

"I thought you must be. Down here we say 'sick.' I'm Page," she said. "Page Gage."

He was Jarel McDonald.

"Are you Scotch?" she asked.

"Half Scotch and half soda."

Page giggled. "Is that a joke?"

"To some people it is. About Miss Bailey—"

"Peep, we call her. Peep is fine. She's just upset. We were all upset because we thought Uncle Oliver was dead, and then when he wasn't, that all his bones were broken. And Aunt Florrie fainted in the ambu-lance." She stared at the man standing before her. "Why, you're the one!"

Jarel stared back.

"The one who's come to help me! And it couldn't be better—everyone's gone!" In the next ten minutes she could have him in the water! "Listen—" She trembled. "While you're waiting for Peep would you do me a favor?"

He said he wouldn't wait. He was going to the hospital.

"Oh, don't do that! By the time you're there, they'll be here!" She took hold of his sleeve and began herding him around the side of the house.

"Just give me a minute to run in and make a call and see about the burner. Then I'll bring you iced tea and show you the storehouse where I have my canoe."

He halted, amazed. "What's all this paint?" White paint everywhere. On the grass. On the lawn chairs. On a sleeping cat.

"That's what they were doing. Painting the house."

"Not Miss Bailey!"

"Oh no, not Peep." Page told him quickly how the accident happened, how the neighbor's cat (that cat right there) got between Peep's feet when she was bringing out ice water and how Peep threw the water on Aunt Florrie's back, causing her to jiggle the ladder Uncle Oliver was climbing with a fresh can of paint. "Luckily," she said, " he landed on peat moss in the flower bed. It only knocked his breath out. But they're doing X-rays. Just to be sure."

*   *   *

Jarel McDonald (Gerald, Page called him even after he corrected her) was glad to have the iced tea and wanted time to drink it. He needed to get himself ready to meet for the first time his Great-aunt Peep—his benefactress, he would address her—without whom (without which?) he could not have gone to college or bought a new suit or a bus ticket to Houston, Texas. Without whom, without which, he wouldn't be anything.

But this girl, Page, was like ants were biting her, wanting to show him a storehouse and a canoe she had in it, and then wanting him to get it down, which he did balk at because this was the South and slippery ground he was standing on: this young girl in a white neighborhood with nobody around while he was fooling with a boat that didn't belong to him.

"You want me to carry it down to the river?"

"The Little Hunky. I want us to carry it."

"I think you better wait until your uncle gets back."

"But that's why I want to, don't you see?" She had thought of this, putting ice in his glass. "He and I were going canoeing and now he'll be stiff from falling off the ladder and will still want to go, but he won't be able to carry it down."

Well, all right. He guessed he would. He'd take it to the water, but then he was leaving. (He could call Aunt Peep from the bus station and then get out of here before something happened, which he felt up his spine was just about to.)

"If you leave," said Page, "you'll disappoint Miss Bailey."

"She isn't expecting me."

He is selling insurance, Page thought. But it didn't matter why he was there when he was so close to doing what she wanted him to do. On the bank, in fact, of the Little Hunky. Not a beautiful river, but a fast-flowing river this time of year. On a rise, Page noticed, with logs going down it. A scary river that made her remember she might need a weapon.

"Do you have a knife?"

"A knife!" he said.

"Never mind." She tried to swallow, but had no saliva. "My uncle and I, we really have fun out on the river."

Jarel looked at a limb swirling by. "You're taking a chance, riding in a canoe in this kind of water."

"You float in a canoe," Page said. "And it's lovely, just lovely." She turned up her face. "Why don't we try it?"

"Why don't we try jumping off a building?"

"You can swim, can't you?"

Jarel scowled. "Listen girl, you better ask yourself can *you* swim, going fifty miles an hour to the Gulf of Mexico!"

Page laughed. She liked him this way. Loosened up. Sounding more like a boy than the college graduate he claimed to be, up at the storehouse when he laid his coat on his suitcase and took five minutes to smooth the wrinkles out.

"Come on!" she begged now, barely able to breathe with the thrill and the scare of it, all so near. In a minute it could happen.

But he was walking off, leaving, like he said. Before it was done!

"Wait!" she cried. "You have to go with me!"

"I brought the boat down. That's all I'm doing."

"But you're supposed to go! That's why you're here."

He turned around. "I'm here," he said, "to visit a relative."

"You can do that too. You can do it later."

"If you want to go so bad, go by yourself!"

"You think I won't?"

"You're nuts if you do."

"I'm going," she said. "I'm going in this water whether you do or don't." And right in front of him she stepped off the pier.

"Girl!" he cried. "Girl, what are you doing!" He ran to the spot where she had been standing.

She didn't come up.

"Are you drowning down there?"

No bubbles came up.

He jumped in after her.

He had never in his life swum in a river. He was upside down. He was twisted around. *And God Almighty, where was the girl?*

She struck him in the face with arms like oars. She was stuck in the mud, hair streaming from her head in a perfect right angle, hands clutching his ears, grabbing for his shoulders and the cords of his neck.

She was drowning *him!* In a stinking river. In the goddamn South!

His anger saved them. Anger and terror and his young man's strength that kept calling up power from the soles of his feet, generating power in his heart and his brain until he was able to do what he had to do: catch hold of the pier-footings under the water and haul himself out, dragging with him an insane girl with a dead-man's grip on his Adam's apple.

They collapsed on the pier while the Little Hunky River ran out of their clothes.

Jarel lit in at once on Page Gage. "You ruined my suit. My brand new suit!"

She was full of water. Of the memory of water. "Your coat's not ruined."

"I caint go around just wearing a coat!"

"I'm sorry," she said and began to cry.

He was half-crying too. "I'd like to wring your neck instead of these trouser legs. Jumping in that flood! If the mud hadn't caught you, you'd be in Corpus Christi!"

"You're a wonderful swimmer."

"I didn't swim a stroke! You caint swim doodley in that kind of water."

He poured half a cupful out of his shoes. "You caint canoe either. You told a big lie saying you and your uncle were taking that boat out. What you were planning was to have a little fun drowning a black boy."

Page raised her head. "Black boy?" She sat up and looked at him. "Are you delirious?"

"You figured nobody would know if the body floated off, if the jellyfish ate it."

"I was trying to find out how my parents drowned!"

Jarel pulled on his shoes. "Girl, you're the limit."

"They did drown! They drowned right here three years ago. Don't you believe me?"

"I believe you're lying. And if you'd lie about that, you'd lie about anything." He sat up straight. "You'd lie about me." He was cold all at once, colder than he'd been at the bottom of the river. Shivering even, with a vision of bloodhounds licking at his heels. Of newspaper headlines: SWIMMING WITH A WHITE GIRL! ATTEMPTED DROWNING OF WHITE GIRL!!

He leaped to his feet, semihysterical, and ran toward the bluff. "Aunt BoPeep gonna find me in jail!"

Page ran after him. "Who? Peep? Peep is your aunt?"

He grabbed up the wallet he had tossed out to dry. "She spent all that money sending me to college. Now I'm going to the pen!"

"Are you really black?"

"Hell yes, I'm black!"

"You're as white as I am."

"Who's gonna care when they're hanging me?"

"We don't hang people in Garrison County!"

"Since when?"

"Since Civil Rights! You're so smart, surely you've heard of Civil Rights."

"Surely you've heard of Selma, Alabama!"

"Well, you don't have to worry. You saved my life."

"Listen," he said. "I was saving myself. You got saved cuz you were hanging on!"

"You've sure quit sounding like you came from Chicago."

"It don't matter where I came from—it's where I'm going!" He pushed past her. "Down to that bus station and out of here!"

"Are you going down the street in those muddy pants?"

He stopped short and looked at himself.

"If you have another pair, I'll take those to the cleaners."

"How's any cleaners going to help me now?"

"Gerald—"

"*Jarel!*"

"It's too late anyway. Look up yonder."

He looked toward the bluff. Three persons were looking at him.

"Peep and Aunt Florrie," Page said. "And that's Uncle Oliver all stooped over." Page waved her arms. "Don't come down. We're coming up."

"I'm not coming up!"

"Where are you going, Gerald? Back in the river?"

Jarel stayed overnight and ate supper at the table with Page, Oliver and Florrie and supposedly Peep, but she never sat at her place. She went to and fro, kitchen to dining room and back again.

Florrie's voice fluttered over them with snippets from poems mixed with subdued little silences when she pictured Oliver lying lifeless in the flower bed.

Page was required to tell once more what crazy notion made her jump in the river. When she got to the reason, they cried again—all except Jarel—as they had on the lawn when they heard it the first time.

Jarel was the centerpiece, the golden hero with a college degree. They couldn't stop looking at him: a black man, yet not a black man, strange even to Peep since all his life his mother, Odessa, had sent her aunt pictures of a black boy growing up (a neighborhood boy), the reason being (Jarel said in his best Chicago diction) that nobody was sure if Aunt BoPeep would spend her money educating a white boy.

Then he was embarrassed and Florrie said, "But of course she would have."

"She might not would have," Peep announced, bringing in bread pudding with currant jelly to spread on top. "Might would have thought a boy as white as Jarel could look after himself."

A mauve color came up Jarel's neck. "I always had jobs." He had calmed down some, but he still had the shakes.

Florrie said soothingly, "And now you have a new job in Houston, Texas, with an important firm."

Page asked across the table, "What will you wear since your suit is ruined?"

"That suit'll be fine," Peep said. She had spent sixty years cleaning white linen suits. "Muddy spots take to milk like kittens."

Oliver was asked if his back was hurting when he said after dessert he was going to bed.

Page said, "You were all bent over up on the bluff."

"I was bent over the evidence of a thief on my property." Oliver winked at Jarel. "Nice white coat and a good-looking suitcase."

"I'm sorry, sir, you found your storeroom open." Jarel glared at Page. "And your canoe missing."

Oliver shook his hand. "You saved my niece. That's all that matters."

He went upstairs then, taking Florrie with him. Peep and Jarel went in the kitchen and shut the door. Left by herself, Page sat on the bluff and watched the Little Hunky with moonlight on it.

In the morning Page said to Jarel while Peep was at her house putting on her hat for the ride to the bus station, "It was nice of you yesterday to pull me out of the river."

"It was the farthest thing from nice I ever did."

"I think I might marry you."

"Girl!" he said. "You are truly crazy!"

"Anna Catherine is my name if you'd like to write me."

"I would not like to write you! Or ever see you again!"

"Oh, but you will. You saved my life, so you have to look after me until I die." He backed wall-eyed into the china closet.

"Grandfather Gage left Peep an inheritance because naming her was the same thing as saving her life. She had a claim on him. He put it in his will. If you have a will, you could put it in yours."

"You listen to me!"

"Gerald," she said, "will we have black children?"

The bus came early, which it never had, but even before it came into view Jarel said his good-byes and went to stand at the station door, bag in hand.

"Facing east," said Oliver, "toward his first big job."

"In the Exprason Building," Peep said.

"Esperson," said Oliver, watching regretfully as Jarel boarded. "I wish I could have kept him to work at the Yard." Jarel's accounting degree hung on Peep's wall in a nice gold frame he pulled out of his suitcase before supper. "He's a smart young man."

"Kinda jittery though," Peep brooded.

"A lot happened to him when he stopped off in Garrison. And naturally he's skittish about living in the South. But he'll be all right. Everybody starting out has to worry about something."

"And some does that ain't startin out."

"Does the last word always have to be yours?"

Peep waved at the bus. "There he go." She turned to Oliver. "You jittery too."

Oliver sighed. "Last night I had a long talk with Florrie. I told her everything. About T. G. About the trouble at the Yard."

"You musta jarred somethin loose when you fell off the ladder."

"Anna Catherine jarred me, almost drowning herself. Imagine that child, carrying around such an idea." He cleared his throat. "And Florrie too. Florrie had a surprise."

"Uh-oh. Do she got a lover hidin in the closet?"

"Florrie confessed that when we first married, her biggest dream was to work at the Yard. To work at my side."

"I said she had starch! It just needed sprinkling."

"She never wanted to be a poet, trailing around in pajamas and scarves."

"She like it pretty good now."

"She made the most of it, but back at the start what she really wanted was a job at the lumberyard. When she saw I'd be against having her work, she turned literary to distinguish herself in some kind of way from the ladies with the know-how for giving teas and joining clubs."

"Miz Florrie," said Peep. "Keep her out of my kitchen."

"She wants to work at the Yard now and help me out of this fix."

"We saw yesterday what a help she can be."

"I appreciate it," Oliver said, "but her poet job has taken over now. And it wouldn't do to let the county down."

"She going along with that?"

"Said she would, but she's worried about the money."

"You aint, a-course. You got plenty money."

Oliver started the car. "I see where you're heading and we're not going there."

She attempted regularly to give him her inheritance. "What do I need money for?"

"To support your relatives." Oliver backed into the street. "Look at what you were able to do for Jarel."

"And for all those cousins I bailed out of jail. Been a pity, wouldn't it, if they'd had to straighten up and take care of theirselves."

"There is no way, Peep, I will ever risk losing what my father left you. Now tell me what you need at the grocery store."

"I don't buy groceries on the Lord's Day." She set her hat straight. "Drive around town. Less look at houses. How you like that yeller one over there?"

"I don't like it. Houses ought to be white."

"Uh-huh. Like only white folks is the ones can have money and everbody else got to borry from them."

"Oh, I see. Now I'd be borrowing."

"You was always borrowing. I took that for granite."

"And if I couldn't pay you back?"

"I wouldn't die till you did."

Oliver said crossly, "Stop meddling, Peep. I'll get my house painted in my own time."

"No way Miz Florrie ever gonna let you up a ladder again. And what about the gutters falling off? And the boards in the hall about to go through?"

Oliver stopped Princess Pat at a green light. "I know you love me. I know you would do anything to help me out, but I cannot take your money, borrowed or not. It goes against everything I ever knew about anything."

"Better move on," Peep said placidly, "or Old Jed Thompson gonna honk you on."

Further down the street she commented mildly, "Start out small."

"Peep, dammit!"

"Borry just enough to shape up the house. Then borry a little more to fix up the Yard. Nobody got to know except you and me."

"I am goddamned tired of keeping secrets."

"Then put it in the paper." She grinned widely. "Wouldn't be no worse than *Gator Flattened on Friday.*"

"I will not take your money."

"You and your pride gonna wait five years to git your house painted white?"

"Maybe ten."

"Well, me and my pride is painting mine black. Maybe tomorrow." She reached for the armrest. "You gonna wreck your car if you don't watch out."

"Whoever heard of a house painted *black*?"

"In two or three days, everbody living in Garrison County."

"I won't stand for it, Peep."

"Didn't figure you would." She sighed with contentment. "Whenever it suits you, we'll draw up the papers."

Page came into the kitchen at a quarter to five. "Is it still Sunday?"

"You'd know," Peep said, "if you had to fix supper and you was still tired from fixin dinner."

"I'll cook. I'll have biscuits and eggs."

Peep sat in her rocker. "Go on and do it."

"Would you really let me?"

"I'm thinkin about it."

Page sat on her stool. "I'm Anna Catherine again."

"You always was."

"I mean I'm through with being Page. I was hiding then."

"Is that a fact?"

Anna Catherine put her head in BoPeep's lap. "Did you know all along? Did everyone know?"

"More or less. Reach me my piller."

"Don't go to sleep. I want to tell you something."

"Is the burner still goin under the coffeepot?"

Anna Catherine turned it off. "I think I've caught on to the boyfriend business. You scare them, that's all. Men are very attracted to frightening situations."

"Like rats to traps?"

"Traps are too final. This is more like bait."

"You been baiting some boy?"

"Your nephew," Anna Catherine said, watching her closely. "I scared him at the river, and I scared him really bad in the dining room."

Peep rocked. "Didn't seem to me he was too took with you."

"He was, though, and he'll be back. In just a few weeks when he gets his first check and has a little money to take me out."

"The one you be scaring with this kind of talk is your Uncle Oliver. Jarel look white, but he black as can be."

"I don't care about that."

"There's them that does. And one other thing." Peep gazed at the ceiling. "He 'bout to git married."

"He is not, Peep!"

"Sure is. She Japanese."

"You're making that up."

"She a little bitty thing. A tap dancer."

Anna Catherine went to the window and looked out. "I knew you wouldn't like it. And now you're lying to me. You lie to me a lot and when I get older I'm going to hold it against you."

"You cryin?"

"I'm looking at the daylilies."

"There's boys around here heard about you jumpin in the river and they's so scared they caint do nothing but hunt for your number in the telephone book."

Anna Catherine faced Peep. "That's another lie."

"I knew one of em's name. Let me think."

"Russ? Was it Russ?"

"Russ. That's it."

A native Texan, ANNETTE SANFORD taught high school English for a quarter of a century before becoming a full-time writer in the mid-1970s. Her first collection, *Lasting Attachments*, published in 1989 by SMU Press, was received with much critical acclaim and was given the Southwest Booksellers–*Dallas Times-Herald* fiction award. Her stories have been featured on National Public Radio and have been read  in live performance at Symphony Space literary events in New York City, and as part of the Texas Bound Literary Series in Dallas and around the state. Her stories have been widely published in many venues, including *McCall's, Redbook, The North American Review, The Ohio Review,* and *Southwest Review*; they've been anthologized in such places as *Best American Short Stories; New Stories from the South, The Year's Best* (1988, 1989, 1993, and 1998); and *New Fiction from New England, 1986.*

The recipient of two fellowships from the National Endowment for the Arts, Sanford received a Texas Commission on the Arts Writers Recognition Award in 1981. She currently pursues her own writing projects and reviews books for *The Dallas Morning News* from her writing studio behind her home in Ganado, Texas.